Eoghan Smith

The
Failing
Heart

D1331862

Dedalus

Published in the UK by Dedalus Limited,
24-26, St Judith's Lane, Sawtry, Cambs, PE28 5XE
email: info@dedalusbooks.com
www.dedalusbooks.com

ISBN printed book 978 1 910213 91 9
ISBN ebook 978 1 912868 00 1

Dedalus is distributed in the USA & Canada by SCB Distributors
15608 South New Century Drive, Gardena, CA 90248
email: info@scbdistributors.com   web: www.scbdistributors.com

Dedalus is distributed in Australia by Peribo Pty Ltd
58, Beaumont Road, Mount Kuring-gai, N.S.W. 2080
email: info@peribo.com.au

First published by Dedalus in 2018

Printed and bound in Great Britain by Clays Ltd, Elcograf S.p.A.
Typeset by Marie Lane

Dedalus Original Fiction in Paperback

ɔghan Smith is an Irish writer, critic and academic. He ɔmpleted a PhD at Maynooth University, and has taught ŋglish literature at universities and colleges in Dublin, Iaynooth and Carlow since the mid-2000s.

Ie is the author of a full-length study of the novels of John ;anville, and the co-editor of a collection of essays on Irish uburban literary and visual cultures. He has contributed ιumerous essays, articles and reviews on literature and visual ;ulture to a variety of academic and literary publications.

The Failing Heart is his first novel.

ONE

He has been here again. I can smell him, taste him in the air. It is now almost eight weeks since I first came to this place – to my place. You might think that after eight weeks I would have become accustomed to these disturbances, but no, I am unsettled once again. This evening I had just put my mind to the question, my question, *the* question, when in he burst, into my flat, demanding his due, snarling about downpayments and contracts, waving his little black book at me in a manner that was less than courteous. I raised a hand to silence him. I told him *Wait, wait, will you wait, I am working*, but it was too late. The chilly, late March damp he brought in with him was poisoned by his noxious aftershave. I wrote haphazardly, in hope, in fear, trying to blacken the page before the words were lost to me. My concentration was sundered, shot through with his presence. I could hear only his body stirring the air behind me. I wrote quicker, trying to ignore him, convinced his breathing became heavier. The more I wrote, the heavier he breathed. I confused the words on the page. I misplaced a conjunction at the beginning of the sentence. I overindulged the subject, and somehow lost the object. In the end it was hopeless: I could no longer ignore the dead weight of his being there.

I let down my pen and rose from the table. Behind me, he had adopted a defiant posture. He squinted furiously and twitched his shoulders. I could see he was jumpy. We both were, as a matter of fact. For a moment I thought I might have to use my fists. I admit the prospect of violence did not make me unhappy, it even excited me a little, made me a little giddy. He rolled his eyes over my bookshelves and turned down the corners of his mouth. He poked his fingers into my last piece of bread. It was not fresh. He snorted cynically. Probing for some evidence of wealth no doubt, some trace of prosperity. Looking for the few miserable pence that I owe him. *My due*, he said, *where is my due?* I opened my empty palms. His fingers left hollows in the bread. A feeling of disgust came over me. He nodded slowly. *Yes I see what's going on here*, he said.

I did not, could not, speak.

I am here for my due, he said.

But, I said, trying to recover my composure, *today is not the due date.*

He did not speak.

You will get your due, but not before time, I added with artificial defiance, trying not to look towards the press where I had stashed my money.

We held each other's stare. The pressure to keep my eyes in place was immense, but eventually he blew out his cheeks and pointed at me again before turning on his heels.

My due, he warned over his shoulder, a half-smile appearing on his face. *I will get my due.* Well let him come, let him look, let him ask his insufferable questions – there are no answers here.

The Failing Heart

He backed out of the flat with painful deliberation, keeping his eye fixed on me through the narrowing gap between the door and the frame. I pressed my ear to the keyhole to hear the sound of his departure. My heart was thrashing wildly inside my chest. When I was sure he had gone, I rushed to the press in the kitchen to check the money was still there, for it might all have been a trick, the whole thing, he might have already stolen in some time when I was sleeping and taken the money, he might have watched me as I slept, he might have taken a pillow in his hand – but no. Stop. The money was still there.

I ran into the living room and packed up my writing things where I had left them scattered and clambered into bed, unable to close my eyes and incapable of keeping them open.

Irregular behaviour, you may think, but you would be wrong. Just two weeks ago, as I was halfway to sleep, I heard the rapping of a ringed finger against the window and threats being shouted through the letterbox. I was already in a state of unease. My deceased mother had been lately infiltrating my dreams; at times I could not be sure whether I was awake or asleep, or for that matter, if she was alive or dead. Sometimes I dreamed that she was dead and sometimes I dreamed that she was alive. Sometimes she was neither dead nor alive but in some unfixed, zombified state in between. On that night I was dreaming of my mother's birth. I was holding my grandmother's hand and urging her to push. Through a frosted glass window, I could see the opaque form of my father in a waiting room, slowly pacing the floor. I had the impression of a troubled look on his face; he kept stroking a moustache that he had acquired from some unknown realm of my unconscious. His fingers were stained a little yellow. There was something distasteful about his mouth, something indecent that revolted me. He was treading back and forth across the threshold of the delivery room; later I would remember how his bad leg was in working order. Several times he was about to come in, but as soon as he put a foot inside he turned abruptly on his heel and strode away, clasping and unclasping his hands behind the long black cloak he was wearing. I could see him better now. A large lotus flower that was hemmed into the breast pocket of his coat was beginning to droop. I appreciate how improbable he was; even as a figure in my dreams he was unlikely. But let's not worry about implausibilities, I have so little faith myself. A dark, red, half-globe was my mother's head struggling out of the womb. I smoothed my grandmother's hair and told her to make one last effort. The midwife shook her head gravely and produced forceps. From somewhere came a high and squealing noise, much like the mew of a hungry kitten. My grandmother scrunched her eyes and began to moan, pulling my head closer to her mouth. It is said that the dead are barred from communicating with the living but this was not true in my dream, not true in any dream. She was whispering something that I couldn't hear. *What is it grandma*, I said, *what do you want to say?* She clutched me by the collar and raised herself up at the same time as she pulled me down. The old crone was stronger than I had thought. Or perhaps I was weaker. Oh for Christ's sake, perhaps it's all the same, it doesn't matter, these details. *What is it grandma,* I repeated. She was shuffling her fingers beneath the bed-sheets in a manner that made me uncomfortable. She was so close now that her tooth decay began to overwhelm my senses. Didn't the old hag ever learn to floss, I found myself asking, look at that repulsive calculus. She produced a hand to reveal a yellow-green lump smeared with red, like a giant snotty nosebleed, or a melted marble. *The mucus plug*, the midwife started shouting, *it's the bloody show!* She clapped her hands in excitement and just then my mother's flat, shut-eyed head started to bulge out of my grandmother. It was all happening much too quickly. The baby's mouth and eyes were smeared with blackish-green meconium. I had an urge to clean its face but was afraid I would smother the child. The midwife gave a small but forceful tug, and the rest of my mother slurped out, blood-blotched purple, wriggling and scrawny. That's not true. She was jaundiced, plump and completely still. My grandmother pulled me closer still, close enough to kiss me. She gasped for air. Her half-breath on my cheek was an aborted sentence. *What is it grandma*, I urged, *what is it? I hope*, she managed to say, *vagitus uterinus… vagitus…* but the rest was lost and never to be regained and at that point the cold sound of the metal ring on the glass put an end to my matrilineal phantoms. I sat bolt upright, my ears pricked. I assumed it was a burglar, skulking about outside the window. I heard the dull sound of a terracotta crash. I recognised it as the pot of sapling geraniums that I had been cultivating clumsily being crushed underfoot. So, not so stealthy, I thought, but potentially dangerous nonetheless. There was nothing for it but to keep the bastard out. I wedged a key between my fingers to poke the burglar's eye and began creeping towards the door.

A new fear suddenly took hold of me: there was no time to dress and the buttons on my pyjama bottoms had long since fallen off, forcing me to hold them up with one hand. Ordinarily, living alone, there were no issues of personal modesty; often I allowed them to slip to the ground when I had to use the toilet, even enjoyed the freedom of it a little. But now I was convinced that my flat was going to be broken into and I was about to be assaulted. I imagined the worst. Should there be a scuffle and were I to be knocked unconscious – being unable to defend myself properly – would they find me humiliated, beaten and robbed, with my pyjamas flying half-mast at my knees. Or worse, around my ankles? Who might find me in this shameful state of undress? In my agitation, I cursed my witlessness in leaving myself so exposed and promised myself I would leave at first light. Yes, I would get the hell out of there, had I not been saying it since the first moment I came to this place? Escape: get the hell out. For Christ's sake, get the hell out. The serrated edges of the key dug into my fingers. I tightened my grip on the pyjama bottoms. He rapped again. I adopted a strong working class accent and barked an obscenity to frighten him off. He rapped louder. I bellowed something defamatory about his family. That must have been a mistake. I had forgotten he had a key. He had begun to let himself in the door when he heard the insult, and stopping, mid-push, fixed me with a glassy eye, and said in a cultured voice, *I hope I have not made an error of judgment with you.*

What kind of existence is this? Am I not, after all, a private citizen? I might have been towelling myself in the living room in front of the large mirror. I might have been painting a nude study of myself. I might, even, have been making love. But no, let's not. Enough of that. *Be aware*, he said, *this property belongs to me. Your living here is temporary.* Then off he went on his loathsome little routine, lifting his eyebrows at me, rubbing his chin, nosing the air. Was he wearing white gloves? Did he run a gloved finger over the windowsill to check for traces of dust? There was something inauspicious about his tone.

Now I will not warn you again that failure to make another subsequent payment may result in the activation of the legal consequences which are outlined in the terms of your lease. And what, may I ask you, will you do then? Would you have me put you out in the street? Would you have me responsible for your homelessness? No no no no no. Would you return to the bosom of your mother? You would not. Would you return to the shelter of your father? You would not. Are not both your parents deceased?

Yes, that is half-true, but I did not correct him.

And what is your occupation may I ask you? Did you not mention something about a school?

Yes, I lied, *that's correct, and they owe me my money.*

Now look here, he said, *I do not believe any more that you are awaiting payment from this school. And what are these pages I see you writing on?* he sneered. *Some type of story teller, are you? Some class of a thinker, are you? I will need, as initially agreed with you, a letter of reference stating your good character and reliability from your place of work. And I am afraid that if this can't be provided I shall have to ask you to leave this flat.*

He raised a triumphant eyebrow. And from where did he get such a preposterous voice?

Growing a moustache are we? he said, referring to an irrepressible smudge of downy hair on my lip.

There's your due, I said, for once having it to hand. *It's all there.*

He didn't bother to disguise his disappointment, nor I my contempt for him.

But let him disturb me, let him disgust me. What do I care about him? What is he but a momentary distraction? If this question is to come, I must have solitude. Yes. I must have stillness. Yes. I must have resolve. Yes. I will persevere until I have found my question, the question that lies even at the dead heart of knowledge. All this I know. All this I accept. And only when I have found the question will it be all over: I will abandon everything and begin again.

I am eyeing the date, you see, for the slow, final trudge down to Schorman, that fellow in the university who is my appointed judge. To arbitrate my work, the sum of my exertions, for the final time, yes, for the final time. His advice has been clear: *Simplify, isolate, you must simplify and isolate.*

Yes. Simplify and isolate until the final time.

And so I did. One night, I left my home in the outer suburbs between the ring road and the foothills of the Dublin mountains, filled as it was with wild and profligate mourning for my mother, who surprised everyone by dying when we were least expecting it. There had been assurances she would live for months, maybe years. She was the first emissary of the dead, the one whose death was the annunciation of all the others. I telephoned Schorman, after the funeral. *Simplify and*

isolate, he urged impatiently. *Do I need to tell you again?*
And so I came here, to this flat, to shed the ballast of emotion,
to unmoor the weight of moods. Here, secreted away from
the excesses of my family and friends to find solitude and
simplicity. With an envelope of money that I stole from my
father, I have hidden myself away to work on the question, my
question, *the* question, for which I have as yet no answer.

My mother died a quick death, give or take an hour of dying,
of that much I am certain. Certain too that it was on a gleaming
Spring morning when the birds were in full throat atop my
father's beloved Silver Queens. She was diseased, yes, but it
was something, I suspect, to do with her heart. She had not
appeared at the customary time to make the breakfast, leaving
the remnants of her family waiting at the table. My father had
been telling my sister and I that my mother had woken in the
night terrified by the dream she had had once again, in which
she felt guilty for a killing, but exactly who was killed and by
whom was a mystery. The dead person had no face, was neither
child nor adult, male nor female, but was only killed. Nobody
knew who it was, and the not-knowing made it worse, and in
an intense flush of conscience, my father surmised, though he
had no proof for the claim, she had wakened, sat bolt upright,
and scrabbled desperately in the sheets for his hand. *Hush*, he
calmed her, *hush. And back off to sleep she went, as if it had
never happened, just like that*, he told us. After the story we
sat silently for a while until he began a conversation about the
light in early springtime, and about how surprising it was in
this weather to witness the fullness of hydrangea bloom, such
vivid blues and reds and purples, such lush greens, such thirst.
It had the makings of a lively discussion, but the talk soon

petered out. After another half an hour had passed, my father began to scratch his head and look accusingly at the ceiling. Puzzled, he got up on a stool and tapped the clock that hung over the sink, trying to start up its stalled hands. *Hydrangeas*, remarked my father, *would make a desert of the earth*. My sister sat hungrily with her hands folded across her bosom, frowning at the sink and probing the inside of her cheek with an exploratory tongue. My belly rumbled. *What's happening?* asked my father. *Perhaps she's gone*, my sister said. *Gone where?* I asked. Nobody ventured an answer. *Away?* I offered. *Could she have gone without our noticing?*

Somebody suggested we search for her. We set off. My sister headed for the pantry; my father made for the only fertile patch of the back garden where my mother had latterly taken to growing her own rhubarb. Her spade, still covered in thick, black muck, lay on the ground. But it was I who discovered her, still in the hymeneal bed where she had been reading a battered copy of *The Double*, sitting up with her head thrown back over the pillows and her fissured mouth wide open. A woollen shawl still covered her white-blue shoulders. A glass of water sat untouched on the dresser. The faint musky scent that she had inherited from my grandfather was stagnant in the air. Her lower lip was curled in under her teeth, her eyes staring contemplatively at the light shade. The stillness made me restless. I called my family together and we stood around the bed. We took turns to aimlessly pat her hand. Her hand was so cold the feeling was unpleasant, but it seemed like the thing to do in the circumstances, even though I didn't want to do it. My sister combed her hair and smeared colour on her cheeks, asserting that *She always liked to put a bit of rouge on her cheeks*. My father was shocked by the claim, and he immediately contested it. I suggested that perhaps she had always used blusher. *Don't you know the difference between simple things?* my sister hissed at me. My father said, *No, she always had a natural rosy glow, always had since she was a bloody girl, and who would know best?* My sister insisted otherwise, laying the colour on thicker until my mother obtained the cheeks of a circus clown. My father pointed his finger at my sister wordlessly. But we all soon grew weary of the dispute and the truth of the matter remained unknown.

My mother's face, contorting minute by minute, began to acquire the careless look of someone in the middle of telling a joke. Someone suggested closing her mouth and her eyes – those dead, green eyes still fixed on the ceiling – but the jaw kept flopping open and the eyelids kept popping up. Defeated in the effort, we left her there agog and agape, her final punchline unspoken. I tried to make a pithy observation about her resilience in death, I mean especially in death – or do I mean even in death? – but my father misinterpreted it as a slight on his own character, and made a jerky, threatening gesture towards his belt, just enough to shut my trap. After that, nobody knew where to look. My father kept peeling back the side of the curtains and spying out on to the street as if he was expecting someone. I could tell he was suppressing the urge to whistle a tune. Even the dog, a primped-up, panicky little Bichon Frise bitch with apparently little or no intelligence, seemed embarrassed. My mother had bought the pup to keep her company in her dotage; now the creature seemed at a loss as to what to do. She wandered about the house, getting under my father's feet until he roared at her to get out of his way. She gawked up paralysed by terror of him. He towered over her, raising his fist and shouting short staccato curses until she ran to a corner of the living room, where she promptly deposited little piles of greenish-brown shit. To teach her to do otherwise, my sister rubbed her nose in a turd and smacked her rump hard. But it was no use. She shat a greater, fouller-smelling turd, lowering her head at her shameful lack of self-control. A sense of generalised ignorance began quickly to spread through my family. We waited for something significant to happen. My quiet little fish, my loyal and golden Virginia, swam quiet circles in her clear plastic bowl. She lifted her mouth to the top of the water and made little desperate gobs as if she were trying to breathe the air before sinking to the bottom. She sucked in delicate slivers of faeces hidden between the blue stones and spat them out again at the side of the bowl. Out of one solitary eye she gazed judiciously at the dog.

I found myself watching the clock expectantly. Someone had forgotten to do the shopping so my sister made pots of tea with the same foul-tasting teabag that had been rescued from the kitchen bin. The tea tasted of onions but I felt under some obligation to drink it. We sipped to the sounds of the boy in the adjoining house batting a tennis ball against a wall over the hornet-fury sound of his father's lawnmower. My father gazed out the kitchen window at my mother's rhubarb. *Big obnoxious looking plants*, he said, *big stupid looking leaves on them. You can't do shag-all with the leaves either, poisonous bloody things. All that vegetation for nothing.* A small cloud of bluebottles gathered at the pane of the patio door, softly thudding their heads against the glass. The sun shone in the cloudless sky. We briefly discussed cremating the corpse. My father telephoned his widowed friends for advice on the matter. Somebody suggested – no, *Swore on their life* – it was more dignified than burial. Another said burning the body would show conviction, *It would leave no one in any doubt.*

We sat around for a while, trying not to think of the vacancy my mother's body was pouring into each moment. Something was stuck in my nose, blocking the airwaves, but I dared not pick at it. My father sat unnaturally upright with his hands in his lap, his eyes twitching at the clinking of my sister's cup on her saucer. An hour or two later, four ashen-faced men in tight black suits appeared, treading slowly down the road to our house. A gleaming black hearse trailed them, taking an excruciating amount of time. Eventually, they arrived. A small man with a red face in a bowler hat got out, followed by the driver in dark glasses, and then a tall man, fiercer and more imposing than the rest. *Mister Flanagan,* said my father, shaking hands with the small man in the bowler hat. *We'll soon have her out of your way and get her all fixed up*, chirped Flanagan. *Where is she?* intoned the tall man, addressing me and not my father. I pointed a finger towards the bedroom. We all traipsed upstairs, me, my father, my sister, Flanagan, the tall man, and the rest of the men in black. Someone pushed the door open and the whole lot of us trailed in and circled round the bed. My mother was still gawking at the ceiling. There was a smell of something that I couldn't quite identify, like oranges or soap. Flanagan shook me firmly by the hand, gazing solemnly into my eyes. *Don't worry*, he assured, *we'll give her a good massage, stretch her out, loosen up those limbs. See those whiskers she has on her face*, he said, warming up, *we'll get them right off, aye, we'll give her a good shave all over.*

Take twenty years off her. We'll have her looking right as rain.
My father watched on, his face cracking with resentment.

The tall man set about directing the others, issuing careful instructions about hoisting the corpse into a coffin they had brought with them. The men in black moved mechanically, lifting and sliding with practised sureness. With the body in the hearse they sped off down the road. I imagined my mother stretched in Flanagan's morgue. A white space under blue lighting, Flanagan sewing up her mouth. I winced at the thought of the needle piercing the underneath of her tongue, just behind the lower teeth until an upside-down tent of flesh would appear on the soft underside of my mother's chin, before it was pushed through in one deft movement, the skin elastically snapping back. The day passed into night. Nothing else happened in the quiet of the house. After a while, I grew into the silence. I felt at peace.

The next evening, with some neighbours loitering on the roadside, the sound of four sets of footsteps on the road began to grow from a feint tapping to an audible trudge. Louder and louder the footsteps grew, until I could not hear any other noise except the slow, measured march of leather on concrete. Behind them, Flanagan's hearse shadowed their progress, the shining silver of the hubcaps revolving with an almost torturous slowness. I felt impatient and I had a need to urinate. Just as the men in black reached the house the hearse pulled up to a stop. Flanagan, the driver and the tall man got out, and with the other four men slid the coffin onto a metal trolley and wheeled my mother up the driveway. Flanagan strode with rehearsed solemnity at the head of the procession, the tall man following behind, staring sternly into the distance.

The neighbours lowered their faces as they passed and clasped their hands loosely in front of their groins. Once inside, the men in black refused my sister's offer of tea and rhubarb tart, and instead set about unscrewing the lid off the box. *Here she is*, said the tall one. Nothing happened. The tall one pointed at the corpse. *Look*, he said, pointing, *look*. I obeyed him, felt compelled to by his cold authority and his red eyes that were blazing into mine. I looked. My mother was unhumanly stiff in the coffin. Her hair had been styled in an unfamiliar page-boy cut. The scar above her eye she had picked up as a child had been filled in with skin-coloured putty. Every stray hair on her face had been removed. For some reason she now looked less of a woman. We stood awkwardly around the body for a few minutes and remarked politely on the quality of the mortician's work.

Well, said Flanagan, who had appeared beside us.

She looks very well, my father said.

Thank you, said Flanagan, pleased. *I do it all myself. Mammy always told me I had the hands of an artist*, he said, turning his hands over this way and that. *I always thought I'd make a good sculptor, but the family business you see… my daddy… things take over, and you don't get the same choices twice, do you?*

Indeed, my father said, *indeed*.

But we soon exhausted that talk and the men in black drifted off somberly, leaving the only sounds in the room my father's wheezy breathing and the banging of Virginia's nose against the side of the bowl.

What do we do now? my sister asked. My father looked confused, and I didn't know how to interpret her question either, how to interpret any question for that matter, so neither of us replied. My sister smoothed the corpse's hair. *There, there*, she said, *there, there.*

Silence fell. My father rubbed his bad leg. He wore the vaguely self-conscious look of a man who was suppressing a fart, and perhaps he was.

And then, in one trembling moment, like a river bursting its banks, my sister's wailing began, a low, slow-mouthed keen that sharpened the air and made everything taste like metal. My father and I glanced at each other helplessly. My sister threw herself to the ground and feigned vomiting convulsions, but no one was convinced, so she gave up. More neighbours, some vague relatives whose names and relation I struggled with, and some inquisitive strangers had assembled outside. I judged by their cheeriness, not a little jealously, that they were in good conversation, perhaps even a little giddy. In haste, in panic, my father threw open the doors of our house, inviting the world to view my mother's corpse and to talk about her life and death. *Come in, come in, she's in there.* People offered condolences and ogled her deteriorating remains. They apologetically offered forms of vitality as their comfort: food, touch, talk. For three days the house was full as curious mourners passed through the living room where Flanagan's men had laid my mother out, feeling the shock of her cold forehead and her rubbery fingers stuck together in one eternal, unyielding prayer. The men thrust their hands at me to shake, the women turned their cheeks for me to kiss. Such intimacy seemed inappropriate to me, considering all the facts. Considering all the facts, I was even a little disgusted, a little queasy. I touched them and was touched, and felt the warmth of their blood firing in their veins, the heat of their breaths on my neck as they leaned in. A big-bosomed neighbour of whom I had once harboured adolescent fantasies pressed her body close to mine. I was convinced I felt her nipples harden. Mine certainly did. It was difficult not to feel aroused and repulsed at the same time. Love, sex and death, they are so much the one instinct for me now. My skin was getting hot and for a moment I feared I would have an erection, but fortunately the embrace didn't last long enough. Or maybe I should have said unfortunately, I have so few these days. People brought food and urged us to eat in abundance. We gorged ourselves on lasagne, casseroles, soups of all descriptions, chicken curries, carrot cake, and cucumber sandwiches. We ate dutifully, growing stout, and besides, there was no food left in the house anyway. My sister gleefully rubbed her tummy after each meal, loudly announcing she *would need to go on a diet after all this*.

Oh yes, we were the picture of health; we had never been fed like this before. I could see bitterness in my sister's eyes when she looked at my mother. So this is what it was to eat! She would no longer be deprived. But everywhere was also the heavy stink of rotting flesh. I could do nothing except sense death on every person. Now I saw people as they themselves would be in time to come: rotting, faceless carcasses. Some day they too would have their blood drained by Flanagan, or his son, or his grandson, or his great-grandson and so on through the generations of Flanagans and the generations of dead people, and an aqueous formaldehyde solution pumped through their arteries, their organs sucked dry and embalmed. With luck, they too would be made a customary spectacle in their own homes. My own friends, those I had once trusted would never die, seemed now to bear no resemblance to the weightless spectres they had been in their childhood; the men had bloated and were leaden-footed, the women heavy-breasted and overgrown. They came up to me and hugged me, crushing their bodies up against mine, offering words, offering touch.

Yes, I see them once again coming now, these old friends, these vivid faces whom I no longer know and have abandoned, once more filling up and then slipping out of the empty nothingness that is the temporal mind. Here they are, as if to populate the living space. There is my first childhood friend Fitzgerald, now a twenty-something-year-old peasant like myself, his babyish face marked with thin white lines, his voice sluggish, as if his tongue had swollen in his mouth. *It's hard to credit*, he babbled over and over, as if it was somehow his misfortune. Cullen, my indifferent rival, is there too, with his hard, fatherly hands, clasping my shoulder and muttering unintelligibly to me, hair growing uncontrollably on his thick arms, and probably, I speculated briefly, on his shoulders and back. Others too, whose names I forget or do not care to remember, others who have been obliterated from memory. And there is Traudl, even little Traudl, my Traudl, her frame itself always a brittle cage. She was fuller if no less fragile, her breasts growing plump with mother's milk, her pregnant belly showing the visible signs of fetal distention. What death-driven creature was growing within? My heart beat faster as she embraced me. She stroked my arm and kissed my mouth, and said that she was sorry, fixing her passionless grey eyes upon me. Beneath her dress I swore I could feel the swell of life kicking in her tiny womb, remorseless stretching of the maculate skin, both inside and out.

*　　　*　　　*

It did not take long before the corpse began to decay. The colours were magnificent. Minute by minute it seemed bruises were growing an ever-darker purple around my mother's eyes. The skin was a custard wax of yellow and white. Her lips had thinned into pale blue in the time it took to finish the evening tea. Flanagan had tried to fashion her features into a look of effortless tranquillity, but the suture that kept her lips together had unravelled. I pulled on the thread to fasten up her mouth again, but it became all tangled up where a botched cavity had been carved out under her nose. I gave in to the temptation to put my finger inside and discovered the red-brown roof of her mouth had a texture like overcooked tuna. My father, cursing his choice of undertaker, tried to push her jaws shut but this only had the effect of slackening them further. All these open mouths, living or dead, they never shut up. Loose threads hung from her gums like laces on an old leather boot. My father kept shaking an envelope of money and shouting angrily *Flanagan the bloody fraud* and he was *damned if he was getting his money.* Well! I should have been in my element. There is nothing I like more to hear about, after all, than the demise of others, what words they gasp, what shape they are contorted into, what face they show to the world at their death. And my mother's passing was no less such an event; that I knew her seemed to be of little consequence. Her death, I told myself, was only one death among all the others. She was now in the same degenerate state as all the other mute things in the world, placidly and imperceptibly atrophying; after all, it is the restive labour of the living which is truly freakish. But my sanguinity did not last long; now the living too seemed to decompose before my eyes. When I looked at them all, the men and women who filled the house, I could see them only in their last days, when their insides would turn against them, when the rasp of their breath would be trapped between lung and throat, when the white sheet would be draped over them and the prayers whispered by the bed, and when their skins would have rotted away and the white gleam of skull and bone lay buried under the wet soil, and all their guts liquefying in the muck, until muck and bone and guts were one, indistinguishable, dissoluble sludge. Now death filled every person with a nameless presence, and every thing was dying.

Gradually, in the days that followed, people stopped calling and we were left alone to clear up the half-eaten crusts wrapped in ripped tin foil that they had brought. At first it was my friends. Fitzgerald stood at the threshold, shaking my hand over-vigorously and wiping tears from his eyes and promising his enduring support. *You and I*, he said, *all these years together, I won't forget you, you can rely on me.* He was telling me he loved me and that he knew what I was going through. He smelled of gin and cigarettes. He began to prattle; he had come through a difficult time himself, that to escape a series of bad headaches, he had taken up on his doctor's advice the hobby of bird-watching. *Gets me out*, he said. *You should get out too, take your mind off things. Come with me.* He had developed a special interest in the rooks, their diet and feeding patterns, their distinctive calls, their nesting rituals. The starkness of their blue-black coats and charcoal beaks terrified him a little, he said, but he admired their intelligence, and he believed them capable of episodes of self-awareness. Whoever said, he concluded, that the extraordinary gift of flight was wasted on birds had not understood the un-human modesty of the natural world. He was spending hours on park benches watching them, taking photos of them to browse over later. The rook was a beautiful, sleek animal, both graceful and dignified with its inky feathers, long and slender. *They were much maligned*, he said decisively, eyeing me straight on, *as a bird*. I thanked him for coming and promised I would go with him soon to the park. That seemed to placate him. *You won't regret it*, he said, *bird-watching is very therapeutic*. I was glad to be shot of him and his meaningless babble. Birds? What the hell did I care about birds? Soon after, the nameless others departed, uttering formulaic phrases before disappearing one by one until it seemed that they never were. Then Traudl too, vanishing at the very moment when I thought to return her kiss. I searched the house, upstairs and downstairs, all in vain, and then at the last moment I just caught sight of her gravid form slinking through the doorframe out to Cullen's waiting car. Gone, as if she had never been. Then all the neighbours; the grave-silent men and the muttering women. Perhaps they stopped because the remainder of my own family had begun to reek of putrefying humanity? No? Perhaps they felt unwelcome. Perhaps they got bored. But we ourselves could not bear to be with each other, nor look each other in the eye for fear we might see a reflection of ourselves.

To get relief from each other's stench, we found ways to divert ourselves in the days and weeks that followed. My father took to sudden bouts of violence. Perhaps, like me, he had assumed that he would be the one to die first. I mean that he assumed the event of his death would come before all the others. Perhaps, I mean. But I do not know what I mean. My sister took to performing perverse sexual acts with strangers she met over the internet which she reported to us at length over the dinner table; fellatio was her specialty. The whole, solid, length of a man, right down the gob, testicles resting on her chin, and even better to let his natural violence dictate the proceedings. One man, she told us, forced her to... but I can't. I took to writing poetry. I worked on a series of sonnets, each inspired by attributes of Traudl, her reticent eyes, her vulnerable throat, her down-soft arms. My mother was there too; oh yes, no doubt about that. Out of death my art would be born, I told myself, noting the baroque tenor of my self-assurance. But it was all an echo of elsewhere and elsewhen, and I couldn't strike the right chord of authenticity. Things did not improve. It was not long before there were wild accusations and incendiary rows about my sister's newfound promiscuity. Enraged, my father declared he would exclude her from his will. When I argued for common sense to prevail, my sister made an even lewder allegation about my writing, for which my father blackened my eye. Both blamed me for creating new difficulties in an already difficult situation, but which difficulties, and to whom I was causing them, was unclear to me. I was more upset than injured by their mutual aggression. Had I not tried to offer a critique of her burgeoning sexuality in light of my mother's death? I suggested they both read the works of a gifted psychoanalyst who I had recently discovered. They misunderstood my suggestion, and accused me of having intellectual motivations. I stood my ground and announced that I had written a poem that would help us to make sense of things. For this, my other eye was blackened. When, in the spirit of reconciliation, I suggested my sister should at least take contraceptive precautions, the soundness of my own judgment was questioned by everyone, not helped, no doubt, by my apparent difficulty in distinguishing sexual deviancy from mental distress. A crisis of conviction ensued. Everything was plunged into uncertainty. There was a lot of speculative talk about God. Life deteriorated.

One evening, my father began to kick the Bichon Frise forcefully in the stomach, chasing after it in a circle around the living room. The dog cried pathetically, wondering why it had been singled out for such treatment. After all, she had not shit for days. The dog was horribly confused. She fled terrified under the table to find some protection, fearing she would be brutally murdered by her master. But my father would not stop, showing a passionate side to his personality I had not known existed. He had never beaten me like that, the bastard. How I had dreamed of him beating me like that. How I still dream of it. He would not stop. His tenacity impressed me. He hauled her out from under the table and held her firmly at the neck. He aimed his bad foot where he supposed the dog's liver to be, or her kidneys, or her bowels, and swung back and forth on his good leg, booting her until she whimpered yelps of defeat. The dog cried. But no, still he would not stop. He wanted decisiveness, to destroy her, to hammer the living dust from her body. My sister heroically threw her ample body down in front of the dog, taking several of the blows in silence while my father roared at her to, *Get the hell out of the way*. My sister cried. My father bellowed. The dog scarpered. I was shocked by their commitment. I ran from the room and escaped upstairs into my bedroom, and flung myself onto the bed where I had spent my childhood erecting images of my future, pulling out the white notepad and pen I always kept under my pillow. I attempted to expunge my feelings by writing out another sonnet but I could not continue after the volta. I nearly choked. Nothing could be written that was not only itself and yet the words were wrong. I could feel the softness of the eiderdown beneath my body and knew what would happen next: the urge to masturbate was overwhelming but I bravely fought against it. Through the floorboards I could hear my father threatening to take his belt to the pair of them. I sat on my bed flicking the stub of the pen between my teeth and staring out past the unruly hydrangeas and clumps of rhubarb in the dusky autumn-coloured garden, and over our neighbours' rooftops, and up at the black clay of the gibbous mountainside beyond where my mother was buried. There, in that small and serene graveyard, the distant sounds of Dublin, the city of her birth, could almost be heard; the barking of lost dogs from the nearby pound, the low, gracious trundling of buses and cars and trucks and trams, and further away, too far to be distinct, the faint clamour of thousands of voices in the streets and in the shops and in the pubs. They went about their business, climbing over and over the granite steps of the flats where she had grown up, up through the highest floors to the new rooftop garden to look upon the unrecognisable city, rising with the mustering smells of cooked meat and newly-washed linen, the echoes of children drifting up, a sudden burst of argument in the half-lit stairwell following up behind those climbers. I closed my eyes and dreamed up her face as she had lain stretched, a yellowy-whitish-green, vacant, and fat in death. And down below I could hear the forsaken weeping of the bereaved, and my father helplessly keening, *My darling girl, O my darling girl.* At that very moment I thought some joy might still be possible; I thought we all might grow closer in the manner that I heard people do at these moments, that we would finally be united in our mutual grief. I entertained a picture of myself scuttling downstairs and throwing my arms around my father, even though I could not abide touching the alpine peaks of his skeletal shoulder blades. But things did not improve and I was left to shoulder a guilt, the source of which I could not properly identify.

The funeral had been a simple affair in the end: Flanagan's men had screwed the lid on the box, carried box and body up the hillside, put the whole lot in a ready-dug hole in the ground and covered everything over with a big, untidy pile of muck. The electroplated brass screws seemed an extravagant touch in the circumstances. And that was the end of the palette of death: whatever beautiful greens and purples and blacks were blossoming on the face in the box would remain forever concealed, until the superfluous canvas of the flesh itself fell away, smaller and smaller, to pieces, to bits, to dust, to atoms. The dwindling band of mourners stood around fiddling fingers and looking at the humpbacked mound. Someone attempted a few bars of a folk song but nobody joined in and the effort soon waned, leaving the few stray notes to float off into the sky. Silence fell. There was nothing more to do.

It was then that Flanagan picked an inopportune moment to ask for his due. My father waved the envelope of money in his face, poked him in the chest and told him, *You're going to have to wait Flanagan you charlatan, you're going to have to wait, the botch job you did on my wife*. A row developed. Voices were raised. Flanagan called my father an ingrate; my father branded Flanagan a crook. It seemed for a moment violence would break out in the graveyard, I began to clench my fists, I began to steel my muscles, but to everyone's relief the tall man eventually stooped down and whispered something in Flanagan's ear. Flanagan nodded his head in agreement. The tall man gazed at my father and my sister, and then he turned his red eyes on me, before calling the men in black together. Then one by one they turned down the hill and Flanagan was driven away, his face dark and vengeful.

After a while we sloped off home to scavenge the last remains of the exsiccating cucumber sandwiches. That was the end of my mother too. All her modest freedoms, the aggregate of her substance, had been destroyed. Yes, the history of her life was the history of a failure. Dumped in the ground, her rotting inscrutable, who could truly say what it had all amounted to?

TWO

Things went on. Nothing ended. Nothing began. I called the university.

My mother is dead, I told Schorman. *I may need some time. The document I owe you, I mean. It might not come in on time.*

There was a minute's silence.

I see, said Schorman. *What was it?*

We are not sure. We think maybe the…

Yes yes yes, he interrupted. *So your mother is dead.*

Yes.

There was more silence and I could hear Schorman lighting up a cigarette. *I could offer you sympathy*, he said eventually, *but what use would that be to you? The document is already late. Set to work. My advice is to simplify*, he said decisively. *And isolate. You must isolate yourself.*

That night, while he slept, I crept into my father's room. I knew what I was looking for. On the locker beside his bed was the envelope of money for Flanagan. I had seen my father put it there after the burial, his eyes flashing and his mouth turned glumly down. How did I see him do that? I followed and watched him, will that suffice for now? I inched forward, one toe at a time, taking care to avoid all the creaky floorboards that I knew so well. The nearer I came to the bed, the quicker my heart beat. I reached for the envelope; a sudden, raspy inhale stopped me dead, but he didn't stir, just gasped out the air until the lungs were collapsed, like the appalling deflation that follows the final breath. I didn't move, just kept my eyes on him. I wanted to silence my heart, it was thumping so loudly. For Christ's sake, stop that heart. If he suddenly woke, what then? My eyes slowly adjusting to the gloom, I peered at him as he lay all swaddled up under a blue blanket. He was sleeping on his back, both arms tucked in by his sides. His breathing was heavy and syncopated, almost desperate, a laboured blowing out of varieties of ssh-noises through the gaps between his teeth. Every so often it seemed he would cease to breathe, and I would lower my ear just a little towards his mouth, even stretch a finger under his nose, even reach for his jugular veins, but then suddenly the blowing would start up again in an irregular, palpitating hurry and I would jump back with relief and surprise. He was a strange looking man, all elbows and knees and stretched skin. Stranger than the creature I have grown into myself I mean, I with my skinny thighs, broad shoulders and fat face, a sloppy composite of my parents' worst features. The egg-top of his head was a smooth and blank whitish-pink poking out from under the covers, but his face was crumpled up like a newborn's, the eyes squeezed tightly shut, the nose and mouth all upstretched as if being pulled towards the forehead by invisible hooks. On his brow were three deep furrows. The collar of his brown and white striped pyjama top loosely covered his flaked and wrinkly neck. Now and then he gurgled and chewed his tongue, as if there was something caught in his throat, a hair, or a piece of fluff, or his windpipe rattled and a sigh came out. He farted softly at least twice that I heard. My mother's pillow had been plumped up beside him, her nightdress neatly folded and laid out.

I gazed at him, scrutinising his shrouded form in the gloom. Who was this man and why was he alive? Something black and scalene was welling up inside me, some rough-hewn obsidian sadness that seemed to discomfit me away from the becalming immediacy of the darkness of my parent's room, and how I was enfolded within that other darkness, how I was worlded by this darkness, and I suddenly thought: I could smother him now. Say he died in his sleep. Say he died of grief. The image came to me. Yes, smother him now like an unwanted infant from another time, a bastard son born of a whore, as in some dreary Victorian novel. My throat was filled with acid. I knew what I had to do. Resolved, I bent slowly over the bed and reached for the pillow; beneath me I could hear my father tossing and I stopped again, halting mid-stretch on my tippy-toes. He shifted again and his back was turned to me. He stretched a hand across the bed and it rested on my mother's pillow. So, thwarted again. Now I would have to grab the pillow from under him and suffocate him in one resolute motion. But a doubt entered my head: although I had the advantage, if for some reason I bungled the job I might not prevail in any ensuing scuffle. I thought of him using his belt on me as a punishment and I became afraid. I hovered over him, prevaricating, and then cursed my prevarications. The figure below appeared to me oddly child-like; his crumpled face, the hairless pate, his little rounded fingers, and all at once I saw him as the baby he once was, and how his own father might have looked on him in his cot with pity and bitterness and

35

love, or even hate. I could not stop my heart from welling up. My courage deserted me. I felt suddenly off-balance. I rocked back on my heels. A floorboard creaked. My blood froze.

Enough fantasising. The old man had not stirred. It was time to leave. I knew what I had come for. I told myself I owed him nothing and to me everything was owed. I made my decision and from this all else would come. I seized the envelope of money without hesitation and closed the door behind me, the only noise a slow whistle piping through my father's nose. This was how I fell into my itinerant life, when I became unfamiliar to myself, someone with a hole in the middle.

Isolate, you must isolate, that's what Schorman said, *you don't need the distractions of others. Isolate your own self, and seize possession of it. Simplify.* Yes. I took with me only the essentials, as much as I could fit in my suitcase, my clothes, my shoes, my books, my notepad, my pens, the envelope of money. I carried Virginia over my shoulder in a clear plastic bag of water tied to the end of a stick. In my haste I had forgotten my laptop, but what of it? I still had my pens, had I not? For good measure I threw my phone into a stream where it sank, presumably, into the mucky bed. Good riddance to them both, and all their incessant demands. Yes, I would do what Schorman said. I would simplify things. I would isolate. Now was the time for action, that much was certain. Now was the time to live. Live, I told myself, and live well. So my mother was dead. That meant nothing to me. I still had my own life, had only ever had my own life. I dashed out of the house and caught the last passing bus of the evening. I was the only passenger. I had small change enough for only half of the fare, so I alighted just as the suburbs began to change from the newer estates into the older parts of the city. I soon realised I had nowhere to go.

I wandered the streets for hours, Ranelagh, Rathmines, Portobello, crossing over and back the canal. When morning came it was not so bad because the days were warm at that time of year, and the afternoon gave cause for hope, but that night it felt bitterly cold. I pressed Virginia's bag close to my chest to keep her water warm. My own need for shelter was overwhelming and I nearly considered returning to my father's house. But no: that was not possible, not now, not with my newfound resolve. I considered sleeping in a hotel, but then I knew I could not afford to waste too much money. Besides, better to fend for myself, I told myself, that's the way to be free! That's more like it, now I'm developing some resolve, some long overdue growth of backbone. Luxury would only give me over to the emptiness of boredom. I moved about from street to street, huddling in shop fronts and church doorways, wrapping my arms around my knees and pulling them in tight to my chest. My father would be looking for me, I knew that with bitter conviction. He had forced me into the world through my mother's womb and had demanded my devotion ever since. Of what consequence was that to me? All life was force and devotion until the moment the heart stopped. The money I had taken was my meagre recompense to provide until that day came closer. I grew afraid when there were passers-by and when there were no passers-by, I grew afraid of animals and noises, I grew afraid of most things, but most of all I was afraid of the tramps and their vicious faces. There was one in particular who I feared most of all, a filthy man no older or younger than myself, who popped up unexpectedly more than once on the same streets as I. There he was, sitting completely still in complete silence reading works of, I don't know, of nineteenth-century Russian literature, the bastard. Only when I passed him did he turn his pale blue eyes on me, a scornful half-smile creasing up the stubbled corners of his purple-stained mouth. I shivered in his presence. But I would not go back; no, there could be no return. Tears started to leak down my cheeks – I have always been a chronic sensualist with little or no self-control – but before I completely sickened myself I took to recalling my mother's dead eyeballs and how the vitreous gel would still, even now, be resisting putrefaction. That gave me something to think about and my own eyes soon dried up.

I strayed over Charlemont Bridge, down the South Circular and Heytesbury Street, lugging my suitcase clumsily behind me. All through the lanes and alleys between The Coombe and the canal I clutched the envelope of money in my hand, never letting it out of my grip. I spotted a piece of paper taped to a lamppost advertising the let of a flat in the area. There was to be a showing that evening. I called at the appointed time and was heartened to find I was the only person waiting. The flat was in an old townhouse down a quiet little turnoff called – call it Ivy Street. Yes. Its gentry past long since faded, the white paintwork on the façade was chipped and weather-stained, and the wood on the upper windows was showing signs of terminal rot. Three worn concrete steps with black metal railings formed a bridge from the street to a black door in the middle of two net-curtained windows. My eyes drifted upwards to the first floor. The three upstairs windows were covered in the same net curtains as the ground floor. I darted my eyes across them over and over until the middle one twitched. A hand pulled back the curtain and a bearded man in a dark suit appeared, half shrouded by the glare of the lamplight on the glass. We peered at each other for a moment but I turned away and thought no more about it.

My flat was, I discovered, to be the half-hidden basement, which I could enter by descending a second set of concrete steps at the corner of the building. The comparative seclusion and the apparent lack of immediate neighbours had their obvious attractions. There is no telling, after all, what kind of people I might be burdened with. Other people, they compel you to learn all about them, demanding you learn their name and hear their story, who their parents were, their worthless pasts, all their ludicrous hopes and dreams. Well to blazes with them; I am mystery enough to myself without having to indulge in the lives of others. I am sick of other people! Yes. I know, I know, you might say that I am foolish. In dying need of company I might have only my own spite. I would bear it. You might say in the cold black of night I might be lashed to the forlorn terror of the self. Oh for God's sake, what excess! From now on I promise no more excess. Perhaps I might welcome the loneliness, yes, and know it as a cruel friend. Perhaps I would spend my days gazing at my face in the mirror, lamenting something I had not known I had lost, or had not known I had had, or I had not known I had any knowledge of knowing if I had lost or had something. And would they then one day find my body mouldering slowly in the room, flies and rats and all sorts of pests feasting on my flesh?

My nerves. I must be suffering with my nerves. Get on with it. I have already got somehow sidetracked into speaking of my mother when I was talking about this fellow and his due.

I took the flat at once, handing over to that fellow, what did he call himself? – the owner? the proprietor? – a wad of Flanagan's cash. No sooner had I given him the money than I became fearful of the proprietor, yes, let's just keep it simple and call him that; I had the feeling of being in a greater obligation to the proprietor than I properly understood. I soon discovered that his habits were unpredictable, his movements mysterious. I would wake up in a state of agitation on the morning of the due date, thinking when, when, when will he arrive? When the hell will he show himself to me? I would feel an urge to get out, get the hell out of the place before he showed. Sometimes I get out, sometimes I don't. Sometimes he catches me on the cusp of flight, and vicious delight twinkles in his eye. I would halt in my step, frozen, while he uncurls his bony fingers with expectant glee. He insists on keeping his own key, you understand, and letting himself in at any time of the day of the due date. And sometimes, not on the due date, but the day after, or two days after, or the day before, or a week after, or six days before, or even once, not at all. This is to keep me in fear, I am sure, of the metallic slide of the key in the lock, to keep me in dread of his odious little book, blackened with monies owing and balances outstanding, each pencil mark carrying a suspicion of my encroaching homelessness, of my destitution, of my demise. First the sticky-taped glasses and then the dripping nose, and the innocent-sounding call, and then that stubby leg snaking its way around the door, and he always in that stuffy brown suit of his, with the yellow tie like a streak of congealed vomit. The air around him smells of something rotting, of dead skin. Dandruff is scattered on his shoulders. Scabs pock his face. He is balding, and carries a tremor in his hand. His nails are uncut and did I once see blood behind his ear? Does he suffer from ichthyosis? Yes, I'm sure I saw some scales hardened on the back of his neck. I believe I can smell disease off him; my nostrils bristle in his company. His body repulses me and I make no secret of it. I refuse to breathe through my nose. I refuse to look him in the face.

Once I asked him if his sickness was contagious.

In turn, he humiliated me by asking if I had seen the latest theatre productions, and then sneered when I had not.

I thought as much, he said disdainfully, snorting like a suckling pig. *Yes. I thought as much. My due*, his blue eyes glittering, *give me my due, what I am owed as the proprietor.* Enough of that. He never called himself that; it was I who made up that name, I don't know why. Tell the truth. Can I for once not tell the plain and simple truth? Call him by his name, or at least by the name that he told me.

His name is Mister King.

We began as we have continued. I do not detect a change, for better or for worse, in my opinion of him. That is, I didn't like the look of Mister King then and I still don't now. Besides, I don't trust men who wear socks with their sandals; there is a touch of the bishop about them. But the one promise I can keep is that that's the last word on priests. He wears his trousers (brown corduroy; high waist; no belt; buttons, no zip) too snug about the groin and then insists on standing too close to me. He places one foot, leg bent at the knee, onto the seat of the chair, and then rocks his groin back and forth so that I am sure I can sense a mustiness wafting from his crotch. Does he treat his other tenants to these delights too, or am I alone to have this privilege? The vociferousness of his breathing is surely no act. Perhaps he is an asthmatic, or suffers from emphysema, or cystic fibrosis? He coughs great balls of phlegm and spits them into my sink. Are these the symptoms, perhaps, of leptospirosis? But yet he is powerfully built. More than once I have heard him attribute his physique to his swimming against the sullen tides of the Liffey. Perhaps. I have concluded that despite his physical afflictions Mister King considers himself a beautiful man. (I admit I admire the authority of his walk.) I imagine he suffers, if that is the word, from priapism. He seems proud of his genitalia and undoubtedly fancies himself a great lover. He draws attention to his teeth by baring them at me, perfectly white and straight, which he flicks with his nails. *See that? Perfect enamel. And never had a filling. Evidence*, he says, *of my superiority to the common biped.*

But I am suspicious of him, with his open-necked shirt and his tight trousers. Perhaps I could have been more attentive, but my need for shelter had impaired my judgement. I could not bear another night in the cold, with the vermin nibbling my shoes and the tramps lurking in the shadows, and Virginia in a sulk in the corner of the bag, and especially not after the savage beating I saw a gang of tramps administering to one of their own, no, not after such instinctive, effortless cruelty. He was there too, my well-read beggar friend, orchestrating the violence, observing sardonically from a distance and saying nothing, smug satisfaction spreading over his face. Mister King flapped his arms about and talked excitedly about contracts; then, like plastic flowers from a conjurer's sleeve, he pulled a ragged yellow-brown pair of men's underpants out from behind the radiator – *disgusting* – and started to tell me about the previous tenants. *Teachers, gone like that,* he said with an abruptly loud snap of his fingers. *Ran out on me one day without paying their due. I found a photo they'd left for me in the wardrobe with a message on the back. Thanks for everything it said, sorry about the rent. We had a flight to catch. One of them was giving me the finger. Jet black hair the pair of them. Americans. God, but they drove me mad, drove me bloody mad. Virgins, I'm sure of it. I found bibles in the bedroom,* he said, *and traces of candlewax everywhere.* He clenched his hands into fists. He sighed. I could see he was full of his own self-pity. A blob of sentiment clouded up one of his eyes. I was sickened to see him whimpering with self-pity, sickened! Nor had I followed at all well his story about the previous tenants or grasped its meaning. A nasty feeling of ignorance came over me. I thought about getting the hell out of there. I could get the hell out before it was too late, before I made a mistake, before all my money was gone. But where else should I go? Where else to start? *Well it's yours if you want it,* he said, licking the lead of his pencil. He moved himself beside me, his commanding crotch an inch from my hip, and with an extravagant flourish thrust the rental contract in front of me. *Take the pencil,* smiled Mister King, *and sign your name on the dotted line.*

What could I do? It was adequate, yes, more than adequate. It was simple. It was isolated. This was what I wanted. I had promised myself I would live, finally live. Here I could shrug off the useless passions of my family and the idle chat of my friends. Fitzgerald and Cullen, even Traudl – well to hell with Traudl and to hell with her unborn. There was nothing there in the living room and kitchen but the fundamentals: a door, a window, a chair, a table, a desk, a wardrobe, a sink, a stove, a fridge, a press, a radiator, a light, a rug, a telephone, a packet of matches, and an Electricity Supply Board box. These objects were more than enough as it was. Simple and isolated: Schorman would approve. I longed to tell him, to whisper it in his ear. A toilet in an adjacent room was not wholly unclean. Despite a greenish tinge of some scum in the hairline cracks, the bowl and bath ceramics appeared to be unbroken. I quickly judged they would not leak. A lone silverfish slithered across the floor. I crushed it underfoot. I ran a cynical hand under the tap but was encouraged to find there lukewarm water. *Immersion*, Mister King said, *takes a half an hour. Here's the switch. You'll get about fifteen minutes out of it. Don't overdo it or you'll boil it up and the element will overheat and the whole shagging place will be down around our ears.* (I do not normally need so long, I thought, having only a puny amount of body to wash). He pointed portentously at the ceiling. *The radiator is on a timer which is controlled upstairs. Comes on after six and goes off around ten. That's included in the rent so don't fiddle with it. You won't be cold in the winter.* He kicked the walls. *The walls are thick. It gets as hot as the fires of hell down here.* In spite of some feint smell, the source of which I could not identify, I was beginning, not disconsolately, to visualise a new life.

I was momentarily dispirited in the bedroom. Someone had torn the curtains from the railing – I imagined a jealous lover in a murderous rage doing brutish violence to silent, stubborn objects, but even still they would not disclose their secrets – and had cast them down where they lay crumpled on a hard mattress-less bed. A single, I noticed with brief disappointment. But I had finished with sex, had I not, finished with the Finns, the Canadians, the Scots, the Americans, the French, the Germans, the Irish. Yes. Finished with them all and finished with Traudl too. I promise that it is the last time I will speak of her. (It's true there have been nights when I dreamed up her grey eyes, her narrow shoulders, her small breasts, the hardened studs of her nipples. I had taken them in my mouth many times and thought now again of them, of we two lying in a meadow, my tongue flicking over the little rubbery bullets on her recumbent chest, my lips encircling the areolas each in turn, kissing them, my hand inevitably reaching between her legs to feel her dampness through the white cloth with my fingers, how she opened her thighs to receive me, encouraging my engorgement, keeping her eyes on me, and then, a fi… Enough of that.) I glanced at where I expected Mister King to be but he was nowhere to be seen. There were some dark splotches on the wall, as if, I thought, someone had been coughing up blood. On the floor were strewn some still-damp grains of rice stained a worrisome shade of pink. Something perilous about that. I thought I detected faintly the smell of a child's vomit. I became uneasy. I felt a presence at my shoulder. Mister King had ghosted up behind me. Did he sense my sudden alarm? He raised an eyebrow at me.

Everything satisfactory? he asked.

Who else lives in the building, I asked.

Who else? repeated Mister King quizzically, *but there is nobody else.*

I saw a man with a beard on the upper floor, I said, *in the middle flat. Dark suit.*

Mister King scrunched up his eyes. *Ah, yes,* he replied absent-mindedly, *he won't be here long. Going soon. Very soon. You will be entirely alone.*

Alone?

Entirely alone.

I cast my eye over the flat. *And who lived here before the Americans?* I asked.

Oh, said Mister King, waving a trivialising hand, *others. A single woman for six months. I don't know what became of her. There was a sick man here for a good while after her, but he has gone to a better place now.*

A world arose in my head. A stertorous grotesque in his bed, indigent, poor and dying, angry at the rotting of his liver, at the blackening of his lungs, hating his sickness for his lack of understanding it. Death had been in this place too. I thought again about bolting, but I steeled myself. What was the grotesque but only an intimation of my own carnivorous imagination? Everything was whispering an anonymous past; but what was it I had set myself to do? Yes, to isolate, and in that isolation to summon myself as I might be. What the past is I cannot say, nor why I have acted as I have, but I might only live until my future confirmed or refuted my original intentions. Who said that? I forget. Dead too, whoever it was. I put my hand against the wall, feeling the coolness of the hard stone. Yes. Here I could be enclosed. I would place the chair in the corner of the room under the window with my back to the sink. I would have natural light, but because it was a basement I would have no view to divert me. Through the window all I could see were the cartoonish legs of hurrying people as they scurried along the street and the occasional dog pissing against the lamppost.

To hell with all the others and to hell with Mister King, I thought, live! Live well! That's what's important, that's what matters. To bloody hell with him and his crotch, I've got work to do, have I not? I paced animatedly around the flat, rubbing my palms together. I stretched out on the bed, testing its resistance. I found an old basin and emptied Virginia and her water into it. She darted about eagerly, banging her nose against the sides. I was concerned she would dash her brains out but eventually she began treading water and grew calm, eyeballing me. She seemed aggrieved at something. I offered her some flakes of fish food and this seemed to change her mood. I sat down on the chair and smoothed my hand across the table. I nearly thumped it with the base of my fist in a sudden fit of enthusiasm. Yes. Here I would create my magnum opus. Yes. Here I would formulate the question. Yes. The fundamentals surely. Yes. I nearly got excited, a little giddy even, but I composed myself and said, *Yes yes yes yes yes, I will take it.* He smiled and comradely clapped me on the back, saying, *Good man good man, I knew I liked the look of you.* We shook hands and I gave him his due, and off he went, swinging his legs widely as he walked.

I got busy immediately. I hid the envelope of money I had stolen from my father in the press in the kitchen inside an empty tub of margarine, thinking no more of it. I put away my clothes and shoes, along with the suitcase, in the wardrobe. Then, once settled, I sat down at the desk and took out my books and writing things. The blank page of the notepad was gleaming white before me. I realised anything could be written. The feeling of unwritten possibilities made me a little dizzy, but not too much. A little nauseous also. I thought about writing a sonnet but the only muses I could summon up were my dead mother and my glutinous, oversexed sister, and the poetic feeling soon wore off. No more procrastination. It was time to work.

It was not long before the old habits returned. I dipped in and out of my books, my philosophies, fictions and sciences, jotting down ideas of interest and thoughts that occurred to me, sometimes crossing out and appending my notes, sometimes scribbling furiously and sometimes pausing to contemplate what I had written, sometimes skimming and tracing the words slowly with a hesitant finger, mouthing a sentence or two or speaking a critical word out aloud, turning and turning a thought over in my mind or standing up and pacing the room as I tried to empty my brain, and then after a few hours of reading, writing and thinking in this way, I wrote:

Who is the thinker behind all my thoughts and how could this thinker be both the thing I seek and the source of my seeking? And might the totality of this thinker's existence be more than the content of his thoughts? And if so, what are the ineliminable features of the world that exist in

relation with and/or external to this thinker? And one set
of thoughts overmastered all: what is the significance of
the finitude of this thinker, the fact of finitude for this
thinker and this fact for the inhabited world apropos all
of the above?

Out of all these questions I would distil just one question, the
question, my question. I sucked on my pen and pondered, and
slowed my breath, and I felt the feint tingling of blood passing
along my veins until it gradually became a blithesome throb.

Days passed. Weeks passed. I was at peace now that I had
put myself to work. Silence from the upstairs; most mysterious.
He neither came nor went. At peace, yes, but not palliated.
I was alive, was that not enough? The old urge came back,
and while I eventually gave in, and tugged and tugged though
nothing came out, the stirring itself was a brief pleasure.
As I scrawled on my notepad I became accustomed to the
silence around me, save for the pen on paper and the turn of
a page. I ate a diet of porridge, raisins, bread and peas, ample
sustenance. Occasionally, feeling satisfied with a morning's or
an afternoon's work, to take a break I strolled the streets where
I had previously wandered. They appeared less hostile, even
welcoming, even bustling with human life.

I bought some blank paper and started writing it out, word
by word, line by line. A document was growing. I was on the
brink, the question was coming. I allowed myself to think of
Schorman receiving my pages, who would want me to see
him at once. He would call me at first light. There would be
no time to waste; he would not be available in the months to
come. I pictured myself barging through his door, smashing

my hand against his desk in excitement, shouting *I've got it, I've got it, there's a masterpiece for you!* A wearied glance at me. A hand pointing me towards a chair. He would lay his pen down, and leafing through the pages, lean back in his chair and smile, a look of cautious pride creeping over his face as he begins to nod slowly. *Yes, Yes. I see... Oh that's marvellous. Marvellous!* And standing up, and coming close to me, clutch me in an intimate, Italianate embrace. The warm smell of shaving soap. A hand clasping my shoulder and stroking my back. A voice muffled against my body, his baritone vibrating against the bones in my chest with the words, *Wonderful boy, my wonderful boy.*

THREE

The document has grown. I am resolute. Let us see Schorman; the time has come.

What to say about Schorman. Let us start, and where else to start – for all things begin and end thus – with his appearance. Schorman is an impressively hairy fellow. Oh I grant, I myself am no stranger to body hair. In the crooks of my ears, I have noticed, feathery wisps of the stuff have inexplicably begun to sprout. The less said about my crotch the better. I can find no plausible explanation for such rampant growth. I asked a fellow attached to the Biology Department but he just raised an eyebrow and clicked his tongue. *Evolution?* he suggested with weary disdain. But Schorman's hair is something wilder, something more animal; it coats him thick and dark all over his body; chest, shoulders and back. This very morning I caught him topless, hastily reaching for his shirt, when in a fit of enthusiasm I burst in on him. I think this upset him, and the more so that I discovered it, for in my company he usually keeps himself buttoned up to the collar.

What the hell are you doing, he roared, *have you no bloody hands to knock with? Can't a fellow have some bloody privacy any more?*

Why he was shirtless in his office was a question lost in mutual embarrassment. I was rooted, transfixed by the black circles of fur around his belly button, the impressive length of it, the sweep of chest-hair that obscured his nipples. I had an urge to examine him. Seeing me wide-eyed, Schorman instinctually covered his breast with his hands. *Get out and don't come back until I bloody well tell you*, he roared. I hurried out, fumbling at the handle and mumbling a half-apology, afraid to look him in the eye. Once outside I distracted myself by trying to guess the origin of the distant keyboard-tapping drifting down the corridor, punctuated by an occasional human grunt. I lingered a few speculative moments tilting my ears this way and that – I am nothing if not alert as a menaced crow - until Schorman snapped open his door and silently beckoned me inside with a single, crooked finger. *Sit down*, he ordered, rubbing the back of his neck and scrunching up his eyes. A blue plastic chair sat sidelong at his desk. In the corner a malnourished rubber plant with long, floppy leaves wore a look of disobedience. A bee buzzed madly on the windowsill before giving up to rest pathetically on the window frame.

You fairly took me by surprise. Never intrude in on me like that.

Neither one of us spoke for some time. The tapping seemed to grow louder in the silence.

He took up the pages that I had sent him and flicked through. A hairy finger traced over some words, pausing to mouth a sentence or two. *I am myself the groundwork of these thoughts...* he whispered. *Indeed.* An eyebrow was raised dramatically. A chin was vigorously scratched.

These pages you sent me, this question of yours... I

wonder… I mean to say…

He stopped and looked me in the eye. Through his shirt I could see the outline of dark whorls of hair. I noticed that his nipples were erect. *I mean to say…*

I shifted in my seat.

That tapping, said Schorman, suddenly cocking an ear and shaking his head, *do you hear it? It goes on and on. The Head of Department,* said Schorman after a pause. *Tap tap tap, all day. Do you know what he's writing? Poetry,* he spat. *It's all he writes. It's all he can write.*

A hmm. A click. A buzz.

Is that so? I said, trying to fill the vacuum of the dust and book-stilled office.

Schorman raised his gaze, staring silently at me down his long nose for a few moments, before returning to the page. He held it up, tracing a finger over a sentence. His black hair was flecked with grey. He put the page down and ran black ink over a word. Without looking up he said, *Oh yes, he was once a very fine scholar. Did groundbreaking work. No doubt about that. We haven't had anything quite so logically efficacious on the dispensation of the human self in a long time, I can tell you. Nothing of his calibre. Such honesty. We had high hopes for you,* he added, without raising his fluttering eyelashes. *Yes. High hopes.* He ran a finger over a sentence, appraising its structure. His eyes narrowed. *He found himself in terrible disputes with his colleagues. They said terrible things. Slanders. His career… It took its toll. One day he just gave up,* he added, his voice softening. *Never a word written or spoken to anyone since. Now all he writes is poetry.* Schorman looked up at me. *Poetry,* he said again, the word unpleasant in his mouth. *There is nothing worse than poetry. It's a dysfunctional form of expression for dysfunctional minds.* He turned his face to the window, picked something out in the distance, and paused to look.

The buzzing had stopped completely. I looked for the bee but it was nowhere to be seen.

High hopes, repeated Schorman, resuming his reading. On went the tapping. Please come to the point. The silence was making me restless.

If you prefer, I said, *I can give you a synopsis…*

Ssh! he ejaculated violently. *Ssh!*

When I first came to the university, I tried to refuse him. I pretended to ignore his advances, his intellectual flattery, the reassuring pressure of his kindly hand steering the ball of my back into his office. But in the end I failed not to be seduced by the bottomless depths of his eyes, those sea-green eyes, and the *mitteleuropäische* feint in his voice. A German, or an Austrian, is he? A Swiss? When I was an undergraduate he had one evening cornered me at a reception and asked me if I had given any thought to the formation of a question. *I have*, I said, I had tentatively begun to think about a question. With a glass of red wine in my hand, a quartered sandwich and some loose chatter about the moral subject and the ideal realm, he ensnared me. *Oh I think you should, I think you should. We need fellows like yourself, and you'd be a great asset to the department. If you can find yourself the right question, I think you could produce some interesting work, some significant work. Yes, a work of some significance. You would be a great asset.* I observed myself agreeing with him. Well, I ask you, would you not like to be an asset? Who would not like to be an asset? Perhaps, after all, I have devalued myself. He ran a hand through the thick hair on his head and smiled madly at me, showing me all his smoke-coloured teeth. *Yes*, I said, *yes, I would like to be an asset. Of course you would*, he said, *we all would like to think of ourselves as assets. I shall talk to the Head of Department about you.*

Schorman's eyes roamed over the pages. Moving quicker through them now. He turned one over. His eye moved slowly across the page, hovering over a word, and then quickly he turned another page without pausing to read, and then another page. I could see his impatience growing. Snort, mpff, pff, sniff. Foot-tapping under his desk, hand on cheek. I found myself searching for the bee. Finally he spoke.

What is this elliptical, hand-written goose-shit you have given me to read?

The elsewhere tapping picked up speed.

Have you no computer to write on?

He stared questioningly at me. My face was on fire. I turned my palms to him helplessly.

Here is what I will tell you, he said. *The only thing more egotistical than self-assuredness is self-doubt. You say you are the groundwork of these thoughts, and from hence you have proceeded to establish your question. But in the end self-knowledge must also involve the acknowledgement of others. And if, for example, inquiring privately to yourself, for yourself, in elucidation of yourself, you reached a conclusion where nothing other than the inquiry itself were to be known, then you might be reasonably accused of suffering from a mental disturbance. On this point I am clear: all truths have a quantity of measure. Falsehoods that are not recognisable as commonplace mistakes are to be regarded as mental disturbances. Are you suffering from a mental disturbance?*

I protested that I was not.

I see mental disturbance in your work. By mental disturbance I do not mean dejection, said Schorman. *I do not mean unhappiness, despair, despondency, abjection, anguish or melancholy. I do not mean moodiness. Nor do I mean insanity, lunacy, psychosis, neurasthenia, derangement, schizophrenia or idiocy. The world is full of people who suffer from these. Full of them. But they are not what we are interested in here. What I mean by mental disturbance is the collapse of practical, functional logic, that is, the submission of exteriority to the tyranny of private feeling. And how, then, can truth be measured, if not against the exterior? Hmm? Well? Are you suffering from a mental disturbance?* he asked again.

He looked me straight in the eye until I was forced to blink. When I opened my eyes he was still gazing at me, lighting a cigarette with a studied and terrifying fierceness.

Give up the joking, he said, *if you want to do good and serious work.* He took a slow drag. *I worry for your state of mind. Simplify. Hone your eye. Have you considered the advantages of living among Muslims, especially where they are most devout? Isolate, you must isolate yourself.* He read my words back to me... *The thinker within a pre-given and inter-relational world of subjects and objects must be more than the content of his or her thought...* He threw the pages down on the desk. *Useless! I've read pages and pages and I'm still no wiser to the point of it. What is the point of it? I can make no sense of it.*

I closed my eyes. *When I wrote it I was thinking of my friend Fitzgerald*, I said, *who is very unhappy and who I fear for, and my mother, who has recently died, and my father, I stole some money, and a woman I know, who is pregnant... I mean...*

What? Don't be preposterous. Can you not be more detached? he interjected. *How can you expect anyone to take you seriously if you are so involved with your subject?*

I don't know, I said, *I mean...*

He waved his hand dismissively, *Yes yes yes yes yes, I see. I mean...*

That's enough! Don't you know when to shut up? he shouted, striking his palm violently against the desk. *They are not important to your work! It matters nothing to me or to anyone if you or anyone else is unhappy or pregnant or dead or dying. You say you seek the fundamentals. Isolate. Simplify. Everything else is a distraction.* He got up from his chair and looked me up and down, taking in my full length, the sunlight glinting on the blades of his lashes. I lengthened my spine. From somewhere the bee began buzzing around his office. Schorman picked up the pages and swiped at it madly, but the bee was too quick. *Think that little bastard is trying to get me*, he snarled, *was sure I felt him on my back earlier. Well I can't say that I can give this work my approval*, he sneered, throwing my pages across his desk to me again. *You'll have to try again*, he said, *there's still too much undisciplined thought, too much of you in it. It circles in on itself. There is no question here, only a series of meaningless speculations and juvenile complaints. I'll keep a copy and send you on my recommendations. Handwriting! I will have to speak to the*

Head of Department about you.

My early morning enthusiasm had waned.

He spoke slowly. *Have you done as I have said? Have you isolated yourself?*

I protested that I had. For close on three months I had devoted myself to the question.

Is that so? Judging by what I have read it would seem to me that you have not, but then what do I know? This whole thing might be an error, he said, a tremor of doubt in his voice. *You don't look well*, he added, *you look like a homeless person.* He looked out of the window and clicked his tongue three times. A short hmm and another click. A hmm. A click. A hmm. A click. *The best strategy, you might find*, he said, *is to learn to sit quietly in a room until it is all over. Begin again. I will be expecting better work from you soon. You can show yourself out.*

I began to ask him a question, but he softened down the hair on his arms and closed over his eyes.

Ssh, he said, a finger to his lips, *ssh...*

There was nothing more to say. I gathered up my pages and left his office. Down the corridor the Head of Department's door was ajar, from where I imagined I could hear the sound of verses being composed. I set out for home.

Some weeks since my visit to Schorman. He is gone on his annual desertion to the Alps with his catamite, or so I imagine. An unusually peaceful period, for which I am glad. No sign of Mister King looking for his due, nor anyone else sniffing about outside, disturbing my much-needed sleep. He would come for me one day, of that I am certain. I did my best not to think of him, nor to fear his sudden intrusions, though at night-time I was terrified of the prospect of him bursting in unannounced. Of my father I continued to think little, save for the lash of his belt. Yes, I thought of that and was scared. I should have killed him when I had the chance. Now he would be out to punish me for what I had done, I saw that with awful clarity. All these people, all their demands, their absences were so like presences for me. But as soon as I thought of his punishments, I would distract myself by trying to identify the source of the mysterious smell I could still detect in the flat, or by counting once again the sum of money left in the envelope, or by working on the question. In this way I did not notice time passing except in those moments when I would suddenly notice the shift in the light as the day fell away. In the evenings, for instance, I became infused with kind of wistfulness that I both welcomed and resented. Watching through my window, or once or twice standing outside when I felt brave enough to do so, I would feel a catch in my throat at sunset every evening as the sun began its slow, beautiful, amber and tangerine descent and the stars began to flicker and glow in the summer sky. I would turn to look up at the constellations, picking out the ones I had been taught by my father as a child, and I would realise once again that the day that had been was irrecoverable, just as the night would be, and the stars in those states and configurations from that angle would be when the sun began its night-obliterating ascent.

Isolate, simplify. But how? And at times I felt terribly lonely; night or day it made no difference. Silence crowded in on me with its multiple, spectral forms. I thought too of my mother's corpse, now several months in the ground, under that sun and under those stars, each day and night both a furthering of forgetting and a closing in of our mutual destiny, and I wondered how advanced her decomposition would be, would the maggots and worms and beetles have turned her to a dry skeleton by now or would she, the coffin having kept the scavengers out, still be a skinsack of liquid and sopping bones, and what, I wondered, remained of her hair and nails and teeth, and then I thought of Traudl and the creature sprouting in her womb that was making a living corpse of its mother and my eyes would sting with tears, though I would not let them fall, not yet. These impressions of death did nothing to stop me consuming, far from it. I spent my money on porridge, raisins, bread and peas, not to mention pens, reams of paper, and Mister King's abominable due. I plundered the junk shops for clothes and even, on a whim, bought a cane to twirl. Yet in spite of all this consumption my body became scrawny: though I ate twice a day, with each passing second the process of shrinking and shedding went on, pound by pound, muscle by muscle, cell by cell; my clothes too, fitting me worse and worse, would soon become ragged. And the envelope of money, squirrelled in the press, grew inevitably thinner day by day, each portion of Mister King's due an exaction of my soul.

One day, rather unpredictably considering the randomness of his movements, Mister King called on the appointed day. I was working on the question, I was on the cusp of a breakthrough, on the verge, I had been putting the past behind me, when I heard the slide of the key in the lock. I put down my pen and prepared for the worst, even turned the nib end around in my hand should I have to use it as a weapon. But Mister

King was unusually cordial, even kind. I noticed that he had had a haircut and that the scabs on his face were improving. Even his scaly neck seemed to have cleared up. In a former manifestation he might even have been a handsome man, a great seducer, but now I was getting a little carried away.

Beautiful day, he chirped, *most splendid sun out there. You should get out, make the most of it. You look a bit pale.*

I was naturally disarmed so I said nothing.

Making progress? he asked.

Some, I said.

Well, said Mister King after a moment, *I can see you are a busy man. Perhaps later.* He sniffed the air. The folds of his nostrils crinkled distastefully. *Well, I won't keep you. I am here for my due.*

I handed him the money; I had the exact sum ready to hand so that he would not see me rummaging in the tub of margarine.

Thank you, thank you, he said, with an exaggerated gesture of his hand. *Good luck with your work,* he wished. He took a long inhale, wrinkling his nose. *You might want to open a window. It smells like death in here.*

I nodded at him. As he left he flashed his eyes around the flat, but this time there was no drama. He wished me a good day and left abruptly. I sat back in my chair and took up my pen.

Peaceful, yes, except for the day the silence was punctuated by an unexpected commotion coming from the upstairs. So he had been there all along, my bearded friend, biding his time. I had been writing a poem, labouring over an image that would not fully appear. All of a sudden I heard helpless, female yelping and the cold-hearted sound of a man using his paws. He shouted a vile word at her, and then more vile words, and viler still, and then I imagined I heard some whimpering, and then a terrifying roar. I sat there, shocked, immobile, stuck out my tongue, put my hands on my crotch and scrunched up my eyes until I began to see stars. Straining myself in this way, I conjured up their embroilment, and a door into the sadistic world above me momentarily opened in my imagination. What wounds was he mercilessly inflicting on her? Was that furious snapping the lash of a whip, or a belt? Were there angry red slashes all across her back and bum, and on the back of her white, cold, goosepimpled thighs? Was she tied to the bed, ropes cutting into her wrists? I heard muffled, confused whimpers, like the sound a puzzled mutt might make when beaten unexpectedly by its master. Was she begging him to *Let go of my hair?* Not tied. Too many thuds. Dragging her through the room, caveman-style, was that his game? Thump-thump-thump, something banging, heels presumably, on the floor. A shriek, a shout. Then a loud crash, a body being flung. More whimpering. This was proper violence, I thought, awakened in the full flourishing of his blood-driven manhood. This was masculine violence that was capricious and volatile and exciting. I sensed an opportunity for action. More than once it crossed my mind to punish him as he was doubtlessly punishing her, and I started for the door, my fists tight, grasped the handle, turned it, and I even put a foot outside the door, until I was unexpectedly halted by loud, explosive laughter and, then, what sounded like absent-minded chatter, going on and on, diminishing gradually, and less and less until there was an awful quiet. I feared the worst, and held my breath, but just then a geriatric wheeze of the rusted bedsprings started up, and, flumping back in my chair and opening my trousers, I obediently fell in with the rhythm of their love-making, working myself hard, wrenching this way and that, indulging the odd stroke, the odd tickling of the sack, but they achieved their orgasms too soon for me. Just as well. I couldn't bear that kind of pleasure, not now, not any more. Exhausted and unspent, I reached for my poetry. I just as quickly abandoned it. Peace descended once more. Time passed.

This evening, there was a resplendent summer's sunset of oranges and pinks. Yes, I know. I tell it anyway. I went outside to stand in the street and watched some starlings roosting in a nearby tree for a while. I could not help but admire the beautiful choreography of their evening dance. Even here, in this unremarkable street, nature, both melancholy and magnificent, could not be escaped. I thought if this was my last day on earth then I would at least have seen this glorious, fleeting sky and some of the diffident creatures that lived beneath it. In this moment, that was enough for me. I went inside and lay down on the bed. I do not know why, but I felt happy.

*   *   *

I stopped working. In the absence of activity, living bred new disorders. One day, I began to pick up very strongly the strange smell in the flat. It was a sort of damp, brownish smell that got stuck on the mucus of the olfactory nerve until even the sweetest aroma was tainted so. I did my best to imagine it was not there, but even the most powerful imagination cannot resist the gathering force of an alien stench. It all started faintly enough, just a hint of something unidentifiable that hung about the air. Just a suggestion, an intimation, perhaps even just a trace. But of what? I tried to ignore it, but the more I did the more I was aware I had chosen to do so, and then I could not but notice it, the result all being that I began to experience the hyper-consciousness of freedom that is the agony of the thinking person. Soon the unfamiliar smell became a familiar one, although I still could only identify it by its unfamiliarity. Whatever that means. But let's not worry about meaning for the moment. What was the source? Something stank to high heaven. A dead rat? I had often thought I heard the scrabbling of horny feet beneath the floorboards. Of movement. Of something furtive, of something – yes – of something trying, yes, trying to listen to *me*. If the stench was coming from anywhere, I decided, it must be coming from the bedroom. I put my nose right up to the stains on the sheets and inhaled deeply. Nothing doing beyond the banal crusty semen patches, dried up swimmers too weak to be producing the pungent stench in the flat. Or was it that the deader semen is, the worse the smell becomes? I resolved to destroy the sheets all the same; I did not like the thought of lying about on my unused midnight emissions, some forgotten erotic dream I had doubtlessly responsible for my slumbering gyrations. A preposterous image of my sleeping self-grinding blindly into the mattress suddenly came to me. Enough of that. I opened the bedside locker and found some juvenile poetic efforts scrawled on some yellowed pages. I read a few lines, but it was too revolting to go on after I came across some plagiarised and unconvincing rot about the power of wakeful recollection. A long shot admittedly, but I took a sniff of the poem anyway, just to be on the safe side. Just a whiff of old paper, oddly comforting, but blameless, aside from the overabundance of emotional energy invested in the imagery. I took it into my head that someone had concealed something foul in some hidden press I had not yet discovered. Mister King? Or my father? The burglar I had been expecting, come at last? How did he get into my flat, the bastard? By Christ, I'll take a hammer to – I wondered for a few moments if I was going mad or if my mind had finally been betrayed by my defective senses. Was I actually suffering from a mental disturbance? I stood still, not moving a muscle. Perhaps there was no stench, and I was inventing it all? But no, there it was, hanging in the air. What was it? My eyes felt suddenly itchy and I felt a burst of energy. I searched the flat, looking in places I had not searched before. I rummaged behind the toilet pipes and sank my hands into the cold cistern, dismantling the ballcock. Nothing. I emptied the presses and tore up the seat cushions, but still could find nothing. The top of the wardrobe yielded nothing except a mouthful of dust on which I nearly choked, and still there was nothing. I searched behind the fridge. Nothing. Nor was there anything lying about beneath the plumbing in the kitchen except a single, forsaken rubber glove.

Disconsolate, I leaned back against the sink and drank a glass of water. I sniffed the tap and plughole. Nothing.

And yet there was no denying it: something stank and stank more so by the day.

Something there. Nothing there. Something reeked. Nothing reeked.

Virginia is dead. I had been dozing, and on waking went to feed her, but there was nothing in the bowl, save for a few scattered stones. At first I thought it was a trick of the light until I looked more closely. The sun was already starting to penetrate through the window. A mossy film was making the bowl reflect murkily – perhaps, I thought, the shade was obscuring her. But no; her usual fuzzy orange glow was an absence and the water was completely still. I laid a hand across my breast. There once again was the old familiar thumping of my heart. I checked the window and the door, but there was no sign of forced entry, no evidence of animal activity, no fecal remains of a cat, no tell-tale feathers of a piscicidal bird floating in the air. Another rat perhaps, or the same one? But I was sure I had poisoned every last rat, and then burnt their bodies too. I shuffled slowly towards the bowl like an embarrassed mourner. A cold dread was belching in my gut. I hovered over the rim and peered in, but no – there was nothing inside of it. I dipped my hand into the bowl. For some reason I had expected the water to be cold and sharp, but it was warm and pleasant. I began sifting furiously through the stones at the bottom of the bowl – they were only half an inch deep – but perhaps, I thought, perhaps, perhaps – oh I don't know what perhaps. Perhaps nothing. Perhaps. The more I disturbed the stones the more the water became murky. Little shards of goldfish poo buffeted against my fingers. I dredged up a solitary, sodden breadcrumb. I pulled out a handful of the stones and let them fall out of the bottom of my fist. One by one they fell away, each one clouding the water and lightening the burden in my hand.

It came to me that my father was somehow responsible. Yes, I thought, he is responsible for everything. Angry at me for giving him the slip and stealing his money, all this is his revenge. Not content to plunge me unbidden into the unbidden world but then to insist on my gratitude and to inflict on me these tortures for taking only what was owed to me? Well that money was mine now. That's all that mattered. Yes, it would be just like him to insist otherwise. But if all that was the case then how did he get in? I ran my fingers over the un-tampered-with window hinges. The door was still locked from the inside. A new proposition came to me. It couldn't be possible that he was still here? My eyes drifted towards the ceiling. Was there a secret attic door that I had overlooked? In a basement?

I cocked an ear.

No sound except the remorseless beating of my heart.

I breathed in and out very slowly.

Yes, somehow my father was responsible. The day I brought her home he had immediately resented her and threatened to pour her down the toilet. And now she was gone, my loyal and golden Virginia. I had been asleep for less than half an hour and would surely have woken if my father had been here. Perhaps, I thought, I am still dreaming, perhaps everything was a dream – had I not been having an excess of dreams of late? I sidled slowly over, peering at the bowl this way and that. Nothing behind the toy plastic castle. I took a step closer. Nothing. And another step. Nothing. Then I felt the dreadful pulpy squelch of something semi-solid being trodden into the carpet. Somewhere in the yellow-white mush, a tiny heart had been crushed into goo. There had been too much water in the bowl; now the only trace of her captivity was the smudge of scales on the rim she had struggled over. I took off my shoe and washed the sole under the hot tap. In my grief I was grateful I had worn it.

Everything was on the verge of disintegration. Everywhere was now redundant corpora. I dumped Virginia's squelched remains in the bin where I had burnt the rats. I did not recognise these failed bodies from the struggling creatures they had been. But, I knew, their vagrant little fates were bound up with my own peculiar existence, but I could not think how, for they meant nothing to me. I developed headaches. Isolate, simplify; Schorman was wrong, must be wrong. I cursed his name, the disgusting lying worm. It drove me into and not out of myself. Everywhere now harbingers of the dead. My body too, a vehicle of death. I too was becoming exenterated as if I had a cavity in my chest, and yet I seemed at the same time to stick out at all oblique angles, haphazardly projecting out into a miniaturising world with my grotesque, carbuncular presence. This was how I felt my existence, as an unstoppable evacuant, an outstretching thing in ever-enclosing space and time. And still I was overcome by an urge to confess everything, to document it, my whole indefensible life and all my behaviour and urges and thoughts, though I knew, inevitably, there could be no excuses and no apologies, and none that would answer any questions. Days were passing into nights. Everywhere now the excreta of time.

FOUR

I wondered if I had been too hasty in abandoning my family and friends. Perhaps it was not too late. Perhaps everything could be forgiven. Yes, there was still time I decided. There were people I could talk to. I was after all more than the meagre content of my mind; I was one in a world of billions, extending outwards and partaking in the world. I was not, after all, alone. Lonely, yes, but not alone. I called Fitzgerald from the phone in the flat, which I discovered to my relief was still connected. I was going to confess everything to my oldest friend. I was soon disappointed, even a little affronted. He had not even noticed that I had left my father's house, nor got wind that I had stolen the envelope of money. Some friend he was. I began to tell him about the question, and the visit with Schorman, and would he help me, I recalled the promise he had made at the funeral, but I could tell he wasn't listening. Instead, he started warbling on about himself, telling me again about his adventures in bird-watching. He had been making progress, feeling calmer, but one evening as they were quieting down, an unexpected thing happened: a solitary rook he had been watching all day fell dead, stone dead, from a giant beech tree. There was a sudden desperate, feathery hullabaloo amongst the leaves. The body clumsily struck the branches on its way to earth, upsetting the entire rookery. The birds shrieked angrily and flew up in to the sky just as the dead animal hit the ground with a muffled thump. *It was a funny thing*, he said, *none of the other rooks even flinched. One of their number, dead, just like that and the rest of them just nested right back down. Do you know what? They are simply just big, slow-witted brutes whose savage nature precludes them from knowing such savagery as their own nature.* Oh he had seen dead birds before, no doubt about that. Their carcasses sometimes could be found in fields and those who fell on the road were soon squashed, sable and plum-coloured mess of feathers, beaks and guts. They were often hidden there in the ditches and under the trees if you went searching. But this one he had seen fall helplessly through the branches, clattering its tiny head against the wood and the earth. I could hear his voice wobbling with upset. So much for his doctor's advice. His headaches were worsening, and nothing he did could stop the gathering pain. After the bird he had become a little preoccupied with what he kept on referring to as *the transience of things*, so he had taken up reading some works of French and German philosophy. No, he corrected himself, it was the other way around: first had come the preoccupation, and then had come the reading. In the end he was unsure which was the cause and which was the effect. *It was one way or the other*, he said, *it doesn't matter*. He laughed, not a little nastily I thought.

Fitzgerald, I started in response, *I...*

Yes, go on, he urged, *go on. What do you think?*

I think...

But I no longer had the endurance for this and I hung up the phone. No, Fitzgerald would not do for me. He never had; he had never listened to me, the bastard, even as a child. He had only talked, talked endlessly, piled words upon words. The derisory death of a single, solitary bird? Is that all he had to concern him? A fucking crow, what did I care about it, when all of us and all things around us were under this uncounterable condemnation? I was suffocating. Was there to be no escape? Was it not my turn to speak, I had wanted to say to him, will you not let me confess? To pour it all out, the filth of my life, all my guilt, all my hatred, just once, to someone who will listen?

To hell with Fitzgerald; to hell with his birds, living or dead.

*   *   *

All was not lost. There was another. I phoned Schorman with the vague intention of telling him all that had happened since my mother's death. To my surprise he was in his office. I was a little disconcerted truth be told, I had been content just to make the gesture, just to satisfy my conscience, but I bravely persisted now that he was there, and as soon as I started to speak, he simply cut across me impatiently and said: *Enough. I've had quite enough of this. Where is that document? I'm expecting the revised work, which is by now extremely late. Don't make me have to hunt you down. Have you done what I said?* I told him that I had. *Then send me the document*, he ordered dismissively, *people are waiting for you. People are expecting. I have spoken to the Head of Department about you.*

He breathed heavily down the phone. His chest, rising and falling.

I put the phone down. Schorman was right. I knew what I had to do.

Night after night I frantically wrote page after page, piling paper on paper, thought upon thought, and although the pile of paper grew larger, the store of paper grew thinner, so I would buy more reams, until each ream grew thinner and was used up. And each thought too, piled upon other thoughts, was not some new thought-augmented thought, but a thinner one, as though every thought was an emptying out of another, more fuller thought. They taunted me, those blank, white pages; they turned my stomach. But I would not stop, no. Still I wrote, still I went on. I put my pen down on the paper to trace out a word but my hand was held fixed to the spot as if brain and hand belonged to two different people. I conjured up some strength and I scraped the pen along, etching lines through the paper onto the table below. Leave a mark, I thought darkly, any mark. Say you were here. The nib cut through the paper and blunted on the surface below, leaving a smooth groove in the wood. Say this groove is me and that I am the groove, that I and the table are now indelible parts of each other. I thought about writing a poem but I just as soon stopped. Still nothing came, except the image of Fitzgerald's dead bird, hurtling through the air and crashing onto the earth below. I had not seen it, but it was of me now too, polluting my consciousness. The bird would be rotting into the ground by now, carrion insects and fly larvae feeding off the carcass, eating out its blackberry eyes. I sat back, disconsolate. How could I write and think now? Schorman would murder me I was certain, but of what consequence was that, now that death was at every moment consuming me from the inside out? He would be looking for me soon, looking for my answer to the question, the one I had promised. After all, did he not have his own authorities to answer to? Every morning the sun rose steadily and every evening the same puncturing nail-hole stars came out. It was unremitting; not the same day and not the same night, but new ones carrying out their appointed fates, wasting away. Then, one evening, my ink running out leaving a sentence unfinished, my brain seized with disgust and my eyes burning, I swept everything up in my arms and marching outside I threw it all in the metal bin by the front door, ink-stained paper of my thoughts, proofs of the disfigured ideas they once were.

All was not lost. There was another. I telephoned Traudl and hastily arranged to meet her in the park we both knew from our childhood. I know I said I would not mention her again. That's how easily a promise can be broken.

As soon as I left the flat my whole mood lifted. It had been a warm, sunny summer's day; now the evening was starting to encroach and the shadows lengthen ever so perceptibly. I took a bus to the park, picking out all the buildings and places that I knew so well, past the modest houses and shops and churches of Milltown and Windy Arbour, in the direction of the park that was the beginning of the low, unassuming mountains that overlooked the city. These gentle and homely suburban landscapes in the foothills, they had always been the backdrop to my life, and I felt calm, momentarily at peace with myself and the world I inhabited. Once there I got off and breathed deeply the fresh, nature-scented air. I entered the old black gates and followed the path through the forest and over the stone bridge, until I saw once again the lakeside bench beside the wooden pergola and ornamental jetty, all nestled under some willow trees. It was all just as I had remembered it. The decorative, sage-coloured metal railings in front of the water blended harmoniously with the lusher greens and dense browns of the forest behind. Bushes were in full bloom and a modest gathering of lilies was bumping gently against the soft bank where the willow tips stroked the water. Everywhere the air was filled with the living sound of birdsong, thrushes and larks and finches, and others I could not identify. I sat down in the shade and looked out across the lake. Some female mallards drifted past, the evening light catching their iridescent purple-blue speculum feathers. A clutch of bottle-green-headed drakes had gathered elsewhere on the bank, their glossy breasts flashing proudly beneath their collar rings. In spite of myriad flying insects, the whole setting was, I had to admit, very charming, very tranquil. There was a poem in there somewhere. I closed my eyes and let the breeze waft over my face for a few moments. For a few moments I thought of nothing. I brushed some ticklish creature off my cheek, but I was not otherwise disturbed. Traudl was late, so I stood up at the railing to get a closer look at the ducks but they paddled contemptuously away from me. I peered into the water to see if I could see the bottom. The water was unexpectedly turbid. I picked up a pebble and dropped it, but a mushroom of sediment rose up and everything became obscured. A small, speckled frog slid off a lily into the cloudy water with a satisfying plop.

A shuffling noise behind me was Traudl adjusting her dress. I turned to see her and I could feel my heart surging up in the presence of those grey eyes and self-conscious lips. She smiled and kissed me on the cheek and I had an urge to kiss her back on the mouth. I was half-shocked by the hardness of her pregnancy against me and recoiled quickly at the sensation. In the months that had passed her belly had swollen into a tight balloon, an anomalous, little round lump unmatched elsewhere on her body.

You're here. Beautiful day, she said, waving her hand at nothing in particular.

It is, I agreed.

So warm!

How are you, I ventured.

Traudl made small circles with her hand on her belly and smiled again. *We are well*, she said. She rubbed a hand up and down my arm. *Some sickness, some queasiness. Nothing unusual. I'm sorry I had to leave so quickly after your mother's funeral*, she added. Her mouth crumpled in the corners as she spoke, her eyes soft.

Cullen? I asked.

He's fine, she said.

Good. Good. I gestured towards the seat. *Want to sit down?*

My eyes lifted towards the purple and green mountains haphazardly dotted with small patches of woodland. A memory came of a discontinued life. One early clement autumn evening she and I had first made love in those hills. Perhaps we were teenagers, or twenty, or thereabouts. These empirical details, sometimes I lose my grip on them. We had gone there to escape from her father's house, or my father's house, aimlessly wandering up the winding gravel path that led to the summit of Three Rock. On and on we walked, further and further, until the path levelled out and we mounted the brow. We rested there a while. Two tiny figures perched on the giant, carelessly-scattered boulders that crested the mountain-top, we watched the twilight descend over the green and grey city until one by one lights came on and it all shimmered below us in the growing dark. Above us the constellations crept out; Cassiopeia, Andromeda, Auriga. Orion there too, of course, fending of the barely visible horns of Taurus, the first ones I had learned to name. Night after night my father and I had sat on a little white bench in the back garden, picking out... but I can't. They had never looked so bright, Traudl and I remarked prosaically but sincerely, it must have been the clear sky and the remoteness from the city lights. A moon of milk waxed. Peaceful then, in the evening still, under the immense and secretive heavens. Tender then, on those imprudent rocks. I placed one hand on her warm, soft belly and the other round her sun-browned shoulder. Her head rested in the crook of my shoulder and neck. If we spoke again I can't recall about what; it seems better that way, better to be silent. The breeze carried white spores across the grass. Night began to fall around us. In a field somewhere a beast was distantly calling out. When it was time to go home we made our way down the hill, stepping carefully back down the gravel pathway, round the rounding bends, past an abandoned army firing range, past the car park. Near the bottom now. All at once she seized my hand and led me through a gap in the trees to a small glade. She lay down on the spongy bed of the forest floor and invited me towards her. Encircled by moon-silvered trees, I breathed in woodland pine and Traudl's musk and I quickly became engorged. I swore I could feel her trembling as she enfolded me into her silk, and it seemed we grew copious with each other and in need of nothing, our faces luminous, effulgent mirrors gathering back into each other our own outstreaming light. Afterwards, we had lain there, the heat evaporating from our skin, until we were cooled by the air and until innumerable bats flitted around us and the nocturnal world came alive with strange, animal noises.

Have you heard from my father? I asked her.

She said that she had not, but then again why would she have?

No, I suppose not, I said.

I could feel her looking at me. *Is everything alright?* Traudl asked, *you don't look well. You have lost weight.*

She looked tired. Her straw-coloured hair was fuller and covered over the top of her lightly blue-lined eyelids and darkly-pooled eyes. She laid a hand on my arm and her mouth crumpled up, a small vein protruding on her cheek. Yes, older now, and tired with the burden of impending motherhood. Where was that girl who had taken me by the hand through the trees, laughing and nervous and assured, and who encouraged me over and over then and at other times to seed, though no child of ours ever grew there? She brought me on and on, and then at the final moment urged my withdrawal. She only liked to feel my scatterings spurt on her belly or trickle down and dry on her legs, where they would die within hours. A group of flies were gathering nearby and were buzzing madly into each other. Traudl's proximity was making my skin hot and in spite of myself I could feel the old prurient stirring again. I feared I would have an erection. The thought occurred to me that if the child inside her might yet die, or if I could help it to die in some way, or if it could still be fished from the womb, then the future might yet be altered and Traudl might once more take me inside her as she had before. Her forehead was crumpled up with concern, her gaze resting on my hands. My wrist bones were pronounced on the outside, my lower arms white and scrawny. I followed her eyes as they drifted down my chest and fell on my legs. The fabric of my trousers fell away on each side to leave two thin skeletal rods, tied to my frame like abandoned bicycle wheels on a lamppost, as if I was all bone and no muscle, and merely a scaffold for a human being. She put her hand on my forearm and rubbed it. *Are you alright?* she asked again. The touch of her hand was a jolt that took me outside of myself. Though I wanted the stroke of her compassionate fingers, I itched at the excretion of myself through our intermingling skin. I opened my mouth to speak, but no words came out, my jaw flapping up and down. I shuffled my feet and waved my hands vaguely. *What is it?* asked Traudl. *Tell me. Tell me everything.* But the words would not come and I saw myself in that moment as some scabby outgrowth warping all around me as I disintegrated in the airborne dust of evening.

Then all at once, I started up like an old lawnmower motor, coughing and spluttering at first as the cord is yanked, but once up and running gaining momentum and turning over at a furious pace, roaring angrily into the silence, telling her about my mother's corpse and dreams that I had, about the stolen money and how I had thought about killing my father, about the days spent idly wandering the city and the tramps and all the beatings that I had seen and heard, and how I had encountered Mister King and the flat, and how I was scared of Mister King and my father's belt, and of the punishment that might be administered to me. I told her about my poetry and I told her about the question, how I had worked on the question on Schorman's insistence, but that I could not find the answer because I did not yet know what the question was, and Virginia's death and how I had dumped her body and the stench in the flat and how I could not find the source of the stench, and how I had looked, and torn apart the cushions and emptied the presses looking for its source. I told her about Fitzgerald's bird and I talked and talked, piling words upon words, and I asked her to forgive me, for all that I had done, for all my aches and my failures and my desires and my urges, on and on I went, trying to explain myself, until Traudl squeezed my arm tightly and begged me not to say any more. *Stop talking*, she said, sounding hurt, *please stop talking*.

The flies continued to swarm over the water. *Look at you*, Traudl said, *you're skin and bone.* The lake water dabbed at the jetty, leaving bits of foam on the wood. In the distance the mountains changed shades of mauve and green under the shadow of the occasional clouds and bursts of the sun. *You have to start looking after yourself. You have to try and find some way to live properly.* Untouched now by Traudl, I suddenly longed to lean into her again, to press my lips against her neck, her chin, her mouth. I felt the urge to touch her, and more, to once more feel her beneath me, to enter into her. *Come here*, she said. I shifted closer to her, burning for her to animate my sex and hating myself for it. I was an inflamed, clownish aberration, part human, part animal, part will, part mechanism, begging my erection to grow and die at the same time. Anything could happen. A fly careered into my face before joining the cloud on the lake. *Feel*, Traudl said. She took my hand and placed it on her belly. Through the fabric I could feel her hot, tight skin. She took my fingers and rubbed it up and down her front, over the now protruding naval that felt like a misshapen knot. I found myself wanting her to lower my fingers, to run them over her mound, to feel her wetness. Unbearable, stupid cravings; ludicrous, hateful compulsions of my body. Something was dissolving inside me. A small kick then against my hand: the fluid-engulfed child, writhing in the womb, beating its tiny, defiant fists and legs against the impenetrable blood-lined sac. A human, encased in its mother, struggling to get out into the world that will kill it. Shamefaced, pacified and disappointed, my concupiscence humiliated and worn off. Life was outgrowing life, cannibalising and colonising itself. Where once was vacancy now there was abundance. Traudl smiled at me. *Did you feel that?* she asked. All around us things were bursting into the emptiness. *A new life*, she said. *Yes*, I replied, *a new life*. Traudl put her hand on my arm and began to stroke it again. *You have so much to live for*, she said, *keep going*.

As the hour wore on a new calmness descended, and our talk steadied and diminished. I was glad of it. The evening was settling down into itself. Birds began to roost and the cloud of flies swelled further into a fuzzy grey ball of indiscriminate specks and spaces, until one by one the flies vanished from the air. Traudl and I sat on the bench for a while looking out over the lake until the sun set behind the mountains. Then she left and I was alone again. Soon it was time to leave for home as the enormity of the sky grew perceptible once more by the distant fires that were the stars.

FIVE

Time passed. I forgot about Traudl. To hell with her, that's the last I will speak of her. One day, does it matter what day, I decided to go for a walk, to wander the streets for a few hours with no other intention in mind than to wander. The day had begun brightly. Even the stench in the flat seemed not so potent as it had been. From my window the weather seemed favourable. I dressed myself in my blue shirt, blue jeans and brown shoes, a little ragged perhaps, but comfortingly mine. I combed my hair, pausing over the choice of left, centre or right parting before settling on the left. I rubbed the back of a finger over my teeth and dislodged something foul-smelling with my thumbnail. I filled the sink with lukewarm water and splashed my face, patting the skin around the eyes. Cow lashes and crows' feet. Ready now. Presentable. Not the beauty I was once, far from it, a little worn in places, a little bonier, but still presentable. I unexpectedly found a few measly coppers in my trouser pocket. How they had managed to remain there unnoticed is not something I can easily explain. I might not have mentioned the coppers at all but now that I have I can see that I will have to deal with it. But let's ignore all that for the moment, for the sake of convenience. I jiggled the coins in my pocket and thought about buying a packet of raisins to nibble on. Money, grub, fresh air: there seemed grounds to be cheerful. Stepping outside, the world I found outside was not unpleasant. The sun was shining. There was a tender breeze, the only kind of wind I can properly tolerate. In the open of the street I felt liberated. The sun was climbing higher and soon it would be the part of the day when the sun was at its strongest. I closed my eyes and thought of nothing in particular. This was more like living, I said to myself, this was more like life unadulterated. The pleasant rays of the sun beamed down and the unmistakable feeling of happiness came over me. I tapped my cane against the ground, marching with confidence to its satisfying rhythm.

My scheme did not last long. I had gone no further than the corner at the top of Ivy Street when my natural flair for sensing the goaty smell of sweaty armpits kicked in. Such useless talents in the modern world I have been given. I could have been a painter or a musician, I could have been a dancer, I could have a great dancer, a beautiful, elegant dancer – but no, I won't go on about it. Ordure in its rightful place. I immediately identified the owner by the stench. Yes. No mistake about it, I'd recognise that noxious smell anywhere. And there he was, by the bus stop, just sitting cross-kneed with a book, one hand outstretched, the other tracing a skeletal finger across the page, moving his lips over each word. So! At the books again was he? I threw my eyes over the street, looking to avoid passing him, but since there was no other route I could take, it was useless. The filthy bollocks, he has done this deliberately, I thought. He has sought me out to stir up new torments, just as I had become accustomed to the old ones. There was no way around: I would have to pass him. I realised of course I had an opportunity to use my cane, but I resented that I had no better choice in the matter. Closer and closer I came. From twenty feet I could see by the shapes he was mouthing that these were not the words of the Russians. So, I thought, he is done with the Russians! – no more of them, they had nothing more to say to him, was that it? Is that what was going on here? So now he knows too much? That filthy, yellow, coward of a bastard. No, worse than the Russians; this time it was worse than the Russians – this time he was reading the French. And I was not surprised to see him reading the French: it would be just like him to be reading the French, I thought, just exactly like him to start reading the French, now that he is done with the Russians. How dare he read the French! Ten feet away. He was tracing a finger over the print. The sight of it was enough to make a body sick. Sick! Why don't I just finish him off now and be done with him, I thought. A hot rage surged up inside me. Instead of my cane I wished I had brought my kitchen knife; stab him before he and his comrades give me a beating. A man in a pinstriped suit walked by. *Spare change for the homeless?* the beggar droned. The man in the pinstriped suit ignored his plea and spat on the ground. *Filth*, he shouted at the beggar. Five feet. I was close enough now that germs could be exchanged between us. The thoughts of inhaling a mouthful of his breath turned the meagre contents of my stomach. I could feel my breakfast begin to rise. Hair grease and cigarette smoke caught in my nose. The abject little coward; complete and utter vulgarian. My nostrils began to flare involuntarily in a less than flattering manner; I was sure I was drawing attention to myself. My ears were reddening. My crotch was sweating. And yet still he did not acknowledge me. An elderly woman with a crumpled face waiting on a bus dropped a coin into his cup. A foot away. A pigeon pecked fearlessly at a few crumbs scattered about his feet. The bird did not flinch as the beggar petted its head. *Is that you Mister Pooh*, he said tenderly. On sight of this I had to fight the impulse to use my boot on both of them. Animalist! Verminkind! *Missgeburt!* I pictured myself hauling him up by the collar and hurling him against the wall, thrashing his head with the handle of the cane, lacerating his skull, striking him across the face; by Christ I'd teach that louse to read the French. A swift punt to the groin would end his semblance of manhood. I clasped the cane now, gripping it, just lifting it slightly off the ground. Raise your filthy face to me and I will show you the real meaning of suffering, I will punish you, I will show you my power, I will – but he did not look up at me. Instead, he angled his head slowly and turned his pale blue eyes on another figure on the other side of the road.

I followed the beggar's gaze. A cold dread knotted my stomach. A man. Yes, certainly a man. Living, breathing, present. Was that indecent shadow on his lip a moustache? He was wearing a trench coat and a stovepipe hat, but I could see through his disguise. There was no mistaking who it was: my father. He was stopping people. I could see him showing them a scrap of paper, which I assumed was a photograph. I might have been mistaken, there might have been no photograph, but that is of no significance right now. Some shrugged their shoulders at him, others scurried past him waving dismissively. At first I was surprised – surely a coincidence? What business would he have here, in this part of town, if not to search for me? I could feel the beggar's sardonic eyes on me, could almost hear him wipe a dirty hand across his violet smirk. My inner violence intensified but there was no time to turn it on him now. I was in the grip of my dread. Then from somewhere I found strength; shaking off my paralysis, I turned my back on the pair of them and began to hurry the short distance back to my flat, trying my best not to run for fear of drawing attention to myself. My chest was thumping with a terrifying ferocity. Then my heart nearly stopped completely and I came to an abrupt halt. From the bottom of Ivy Street another figure was slowly coming into view: Mister King. I looked back over my shoulder; there was the beggar; beyond him there was my father. I twisted my head around; there was Mister King, and now behind him yet another figure coming into view, a tall man in black, and his finger pointing up the street in the direction of my father. I followed the tall man's outstretched finger, was compelled to, and one last time my head swung back in the opposite direction. To my surprise my father had disappeared, but there, now, immediately present, was the hearse, like a monstrous black slug leaving its deathly slime all over the road, forcing itself into my consciousness. Then the rest of them came, ashen-faced men in black, all trudging down the street in my direction, their dismal paces tapping out the unwanted beat, half-time of my pounding heart.

I reached my building and I scurried down the steps that led to the flat, accidentally kicking the pot of geraniums as I foostered for my key. My only thought was to get the envelope of money and to somehow effect an escape before it was too late. As I thundered though the door I was met with a stench so strong that I was overcome by a wave of nausea. I just about managed to keep down the morning's porridge in my belly, or, rather, through a sheer act of willpower that surprised even me, I defeated the violent spasms in my gullet. I held on to the door and put a foot inside, stubbing my toe in the movement and causing an unwanted reflex whereby my knee rose up at an oblique angle and banged sharply against the doorframe. I gasped in pain, taking in a mouthful of the offensive air. Feeling foolish and sick, I doubled over. A revolt now began in my throat, but I crushed it with a brave swallow. I clung on to the doorframe, pushing one foot forward, and then the other, making progress in this way. Slow progress, yes, but progress nonetheless. The men in black would be halfway up the street by now. Fighting the urge to vomit, I slid a foot forward slowly, but steadily. Then the other, making more progress. Moving this way, I gradually gained the inside. I felt momentarily vindicated until I was forced to breathe; I didn't want to breathe but my will was not strong enough to overcome my natural impulses. I caught a whiff and my knees began to crack and weaken. *Damn you*, I shouted at no one in particular, *damn you, you prick*. Buckling, I collapsed on the floor, face first into the carpet. Immediately I regretted my decision to forgo that morning's cleaning. My mouth was filled with rotting hair and bits of muck that I had been trampling in off the street for the last few weeks. I tasted what I imagined to be bird droppings and something approximating fish-slime; I couldn't bring myself to name precisely what it was. I know what it was but naming it is a different matter altogether. The mixture made a cold, oily paste on my tongue. Try as I might I couldn't help but masticate, to get a sense of the flavours. I got an unexpected and unpleasant taste of salt. Now I was forced to crawl along on the ground. From the floor, I looked up and saw a pen on the edge of the table, teetering precariously, over my head, like the blade of a guillotine. How did it get there, I wondered, how in Christ did it get there? Who left it there? Outraged, I roared at the pen. *Drop or fuck off*, I shouted, *but don't just hang there over my head*. I shouted again, just to feel alive, *Fuck off!* Making this racket made me feel happier, a little excited even, so I let loose some more at the pen, but not too much in case I got giddy or was overheard. With me on the ground under the precipitously balanced pen and the foul paste in my mouth, now coagulating with my spit to make a warm sauce, I made a pretty picture. There was nothing for it but to adjust myself. If the pen wouldn't drop then I would have to just get out of the way. Summoning up all the remaining will I hadn't wasted on fighting my breathing, I crawled in circles around the couch, lifting my head to avoid ingesting more dirt. Unluckily, I crashed my head into the legs of the table. I say unluckily, but luck had nothing to do with it, since I was the one who had arranged things as they were. In fact crashing my head into the leg of the table was inevitable if you look at it from that perspective. My elbows got burned on the carpet. I wore through the last remaining threads on the knees of my trousers circumnavigating the room. I lay down on the ground, for how long I do not know, for a series of eternal presents it seemed. I cowered, waiting, dreading, but nobody came.

Instead, there came the sound of thumping coming from the upstairs. That fellow beating his lover? I hauled myself up. I began to trust my legs once more and tested them by hopping from one leg to the other. I examined the damage to my knee:

some minor bruising only. My elbows were red raw but they would recover. I breathed in deeply, and then deeply again, just to reassure myself that I could still breathe. The stench was overwhelming, but nonetheless the more I could smell the more alive I felt. More thumps from the upstairs. I crept towards the window to see what was happening. There, outside, on the street, the shiny silver hubcaps of the hearse were gleaming in the sunlight. Two of the men in black were standing beside it; one of them dropped a cigarette and crushed it into the ground with purposeful circles of his foot. I adjusted my position to get a better look. The tall man was there too, staring vacantly into the nothingness, leaning carelessly against the hearse. I feared those eyes, those empty, red eyes. A loud thump from the upstairs caught his attention, and he directed his face upwards to what I surmised was the top storey of the building. Neither of the men spoke to the other. More thumping. My eyes drifted too upwards. Now muffled tones reverberating down through the ceiling from the upstairs, voices on the staircase I guessed. Listening harder. Listening for anything. Someone's name being called. I could barely distinguish between the noises though they grew louder and more distinct. I glanced over at the door. I had not closed it when I came in and now it was ajar. I cursed my stupidity but dared not move. The voices were outside now, on the bridge of steps that led from the street to the ground floor door of the building.

Sorry about the smell, I could just make out Mister King saying, *mysterious causes.*

Jesus Christ, said another voice dramatically, *that's the worst I've come across yet. How long has he been stuck up there?*

I'm not sure, said Mister King. *I had not seen him in a number of weeks, perhaps months.*

You didn't collect the rent from him yourself? asked the voice.

We had other arrangements, said Mister King.

There was a pause. *Fine beard on him all the same*, remarked the voice. *Fine beard. It keeps growing, so they say, but I'm not sure myself. After death, I mean.* There was a pause. *My own daddy had a fine beard too. My mammy wasn't keen on it. I tried to grow one, but I couldn't stand the itch. I do hate any sort of an itch, Mister King. No more than yourself, I'm sure*, he added. They were on the street now. The owner of the voice appeared. It was Flanagan. My legs began to quiver. My groin was sweating and I needed to relieve myself. I feared I would wet my trousers. The door. The envelope of money. What if Mister King…? There was no escape.

Through the window I could see Mister King scratching his neck, frowning at Flanagan. He rubbed his hands together and blew something off them.

There'll be an inquest? said Flanagan casually.

Mister King studied Flanagan's face. *An inquest Mister Flanagan?* he asked. *An inquest? The man is dead*, he said darkly, *dead. Now is not the time for talk of inquests Mister Flanagan.*

But the authorities, replied Flanagan firmly, *will want to know.*

Mister King cocked his head and looked up the street. *Authorities? Know? All I know is that he is dead*, he said.

Flanagan gazed at Mister King for a moment and then nodded sagely. *Right you are Mister King, right you are.*

He is dead surely. Coronary, if I had to guess. He gestured towards the tall man. He began waving his hands, guiding other figures in the building who I could not see from my position, rotating his wrists, beckoning them forward. Tapping of sets of footsteps on concrete overhead; one man in black, then two, then three and four, carrying an unremarkable light brown coffin. The tall man walked to the back of the hearse, and opened the hatch. The driver got out and helped the other men in black slide the coffin into the large empty space, and then the hatch was closed. The tall man got into the hearse with the driver and, on his instruction, the other men in black fell into formation and began to slowly march off down the road. Mister King and Flanagan stood looking at the box for a moment. I fixed on their eyes. Was it possible that they had not seen the open door?

What was he? asked Flanagan.

What was he? quizzed Mister King.

What did he do for a living, said Flanagan.

Mister King shook his head and his jaw started to open but my head was swimming and I could not bear to hear the answer. Now was the time for action. I clambered down off the bed and made a bolt for the door with the sole intention of shutting it, but when I got to it I found I could not help but look upwards through the crack one more time at the two men. Flanagan and Mister King were shaking hands.

I'll be in touch, said Flanagan. He started towards the hearse, but halted abruptly, something crossing his mind.

Oh, he said, lowering his face and looking at Mister King from under his eyebrows. *Payment. I can expect it next week?*

Don't worry Mister Flanagan, Mister King said after

a moment, *you will get your due. Matter of fact*, he added contemplatively, *I'm due a little myself.*

When the engine of the hearse started up I seized my moment and shut the door quickly, my hand trembling, an itch in my ear, a shudder in my leg, and went straight for the tub of margarine: the envelope of money was still there. So they had not been here. I quickly counted the contents. Virtually nothing left, yes, nearly gone, but the exact amount I expected, only enough for Mister King. The mysterious coppers were still in my pocket. With the door shut I could no longer hear what was being said so I went back into the bedroom and crawled up onto the bed to get a better view of the street. Everyone was gone. There was no sign of Mister King or the men in black. I craned my neck to see if I could see the beggar or my father but my view was obscured by railings and trees and the angle was all wrong anyway.

Silence now. Activity ended. As if nothing had happened. All other humans gone. Alone in the flat once again. Confined once again. Stillness. Around me objects were carrying on with their undepictable placidity without any shame, without care of my own derisory tedium. A slow but familiar feeling of disgust came over me. A cold, black nausea began to heave up in my gut, making me feel violent and full of hate. Just exactly what sort of existence is this? Had they not seen me? Or had they ignored me? How dare they ignore me, the bastards! And now, all these other insensate things, expecting nothing, anticipating nothing, not even their own disintegration into dust. What was I in the midst of all this? I felt as if I was a pawn, without any real presence.

I rang Schorman. The work was imperfect but soon, very soon, it would be finished. I was sure of it, I was determined. That was what I wanted, to finish, to have it over with. I was on the verge of formulating the question. He would embrace me as if I were his prodigal son, clasp me to his chest and run an admiring hand down my back. I was breathless with anticipation. I stood up with the receiver in one hand and the base of the phone in the other. The number rang and rang, and my eyes were springing with impatience, until eventually it was picked up on the other end. But when his voice started up, a sudden fear gripped me and I could not speak, only breathe into the receiver.

Well? Who is this, Schorman was questioning, *who is there?*

I did not speak. I was sure my heart was beating too loudly.

Who is this, who is there? Schorman was demanding angrily.

I hung up the phone. On a whim I dialled Fitzgerald's number but some woman I did not know answered. She was shouting, *Hello hello* as if she could not hear me. In the background there was the bustle of many people talking and drinking so I shouted down the line, telling her who I was, but she started gabbling wildly down the line. I listened intently, trying to snatch phrases and meanings out of the blather, but I could not bear to hear the words she had to say so I slammed the receiver down to cut her off.

Outside a bird squawked and then just as soon stopped. I stood in the living room and leaned against the wall. Nothing was happening. And then, just then, a moving thing appeared in the extreme left of my field of vision. Another living thing.

Some species of flying insect that I couldn't identify was climbing the same wall I was using to support myself. It had small wings and a large bulbous head that it was cleaning with long, deliberate strokes of its forearms. We stopped to examine each other. Thousands of black eye-pods fixed on me. Optically outnumbered, I made up for it in size. In that moment, anything might have happened. We both stood still in our positions, neither of us moving. I had the feeling that I had forgotten something important. I knew one of us had to do something, to keep the whole thing going. There were a number of choices. In the end, I smashed my hand against the insect, squashing the little fellow between palm and wall. I almost impressed myself by this act of human power. Does that sound trivial? Let it stand in judgment. The insect was only a tiny, inconsequential thing, a house-pest, a presumably purposeless creature caught unhappily at that instance in the machinery of my mood and movements, an unfortunately placed collection of cells temporarily arranged insect-wise, hardly anything in the cosmic scheme, hardly what could be called a life at all, hardly worth mentioning, but I had destroyed it all the same, and the only unified being it would ever have would now disperse, not immediately but eventually, in one week or two, or perhaps one month or more, I don't know, I don't know these things, into millions of unseen, disparate atoms, until they became part of some other entity, animate or inanimate, no one would know, no one would question. Consolation for I am not sure who. The wings were mashed into the side of my palm, its body spattered on the wall. Delicate, detachable, all in all. Strange to think the insect had had a mother and father, deceased in all probability. Strange to think the insect, male or female or whatever it was, no matter what it was, may have had offspring of its own, perhaps some living, perhaps some dead. On the whole my victory over the wretched creature seemed a little hollow considering it was only a single insect of millions of its kind. But that was not that point, I told myself, that was not the point at all. Truly dead? I prodded it with a finger but the remains just peeled pathetically off the wall and wafted down to the floor. So, it was truly dead. On the soles of my shoes, thousands of deaths, scraped off on the mat unremarked. Killing is simple, I realised. It only takes a little blood-letting and a sense of purpose. Or do I mean no sense of purpose? Either will do just as well: all you need is the heart for it. Inspired so, I resolved to put an end to myself for once and for all. There had been enough bloody fooling around to last, well, to last a lifetime. *Enough is enough*, I said out loud. Decide. Here I was suffering from persistent smells, when the cure was to eliminate the smeller; here I was labouring to find the question, when the answer was to destroy the questioner. I had forgotten whether I still trusted my legs, but it didn't matter: I leapt up and raced to the kitchen and pulled the sharpest knife from the drawer. I tested the blade on the corpse of the insect, slicing it in two. Nothing came out, I had expected something to ooze out, the knife was good and sharp, but there was nothing inside.

I pricked up an ear. No sound from the outside. So I would die alone, just as my mother had died alone, just as everyone dies. That was to be our fate: have done with it if it must be done. How could I imagine my death? I could not be an actor and spectator at the same time, but I imagined it nonetheless. A perfect death, a total death, one where actor and spectator perish together. And they would find my corpse, the last expression my face had contorted into, the one I would never see myself, the one I had always most wanted to see, only ever wanted to see, and all my flesh rotting away and decaying into a messy sludge on the carpet, a clarion to the gathering maggots, and the glorious colours changing minute by minute with no human witness to capture or recoil or revel, surrounded only by all the mute and silent things that sat amidst this deathly and irrefutable being. Am I being romantic? Let me, this once. Have done with it, end it for once and for all. End this torment, this unspeakable endurance. There was only one place to do it. I filled the bath with water and took off all my clothes. *That's it*, I said to myself, *that's more like it! Immerse yourself. Now we're getting somewhere, making real progress, making meaningful progress.* The hot water stung my bum, making me leap up in pain. Well, I thought as I scratched and clenched furiously, that's no good, if you can't stand a little heat on your bum, a little scolding of the rectum, how will you put an end to yourself? Do it, for Christ's sake, die. Father where are you? Mother protect me. I pressed the edge of the knife against my wrist, and considered whether to cut lengthways or sideways. Sideways would seem to be the convention, I'd dreamed up enough melodramas to know that. The blade gleamed under the yellow bulb. The sideways cut would slice open more arteries, but the lengthways cut would bleed me quicker. Precision or speed, that was always my dilemma. I pressed the blade to my wrists, and pressed again, and a little blood dribbled out, but there was no pain, and more than anything I had wanted there to be pain, just so I could feel alive for one last time in that singularity. Let the heart be drained of its blood, let the body carry out its fate and pump itself to death. We are all killers in the end, one way or another. I pressed the knife in further and this time the pain was the agony of self-annihilation made manifest. To die was to never feel the heart beat out each new, pure moment. Everything dead belonged to the past and to the future. If I pressed the knife harder, I would soon be one of them. Death was in my feet and my legs, in my arms and chest and head, in my skin and nails and eyes and hair, in my belly and in my semen, death was a tapeworm, consuming me from the inside out, swallowing out holes in my flesh and distending out into the unwelcoming world through my nose and fingers and toes, into everything I touched and saw and smelled. Hot, absurd tears sprang from my eyes. I had never wanted to die so much as I did in that instance and I had never so much wanted to live. Live, I had told myself, and live well. But how? What use was that to me? The present was here, now; death was the melting wax inside me but this suffering was radiant intensity. My mother was soothing me, stroking my cheek and hushing me to sleep; my father was standing on the landing waiting for my breathing to slow. My parents, my killers. Lovers too: once the thumping in my heart was the tumult of love's hammering, as if something was trying to smash out through the walls of my heart; once I feared my heart might hammer Traudl to death, and if she died that hammering would not stop, but hammer on until I had hammered myself to death. Children too: there was something else inside Traudl now, something vital and desperate that grew out of the death of all human stirring. Those tiny fists were beating within her, beating at the skin they lay within, the blood beating a pulse within those tiny fists. I was reaching deep inside her gaping womb and pulling that puny creature towards me, and holding it before it died, to feel against my chest the failing heart that I knew would not endure. Yes. I knew that. I saw it clearly. I dropped the knife on the floor and ran my arm under the tap. The blood ran with the water down the white ceramic, down the plughole and further down into the sewerage. I looked down at myself and saw my naked body, a useless, superfluous object that did not contain within it the will to go on living or the power to self-destruct. I climbed out of the bath and wrapped a towel around my arm to stop the bleeding. I lay down on the floor of the bathroom, gazing at a fly crawling on the ceiling. One of us was upside down, but whom? And still, over the rising steam, I caught once again a trace of the lingering stench as I breathed in once again the foul air.

*   *   *

And then: this evening, an intrusion, the one I have been waiting for all along. And when it came, it came as I had pictured it. Slow-moving fall of leather by the window; dampened hush of wet leaves underfoot. A human toe clumsily poking the pot of geraniums. A rustle from the bush was the sound of sparrows taking flight. A muffled sneeze, an uncertain brass tapping, a hesitant fingering of the letter-box flap. Yes. So, finally, it had come to this. I downed the pen I had taken up again and turned over my pages. I stood up, buttoned up my trousers and fastened my belt. I put a tea towel over Virginia's empty bowl, not having had the spirit to empty it since her demise. Foot-tap now on concrete, closer tapping now, and closer tapping still until the tapping stopped. I put my ear to the door. Yes. A presence there. My heart began thumping, too loudly I thought, loud enough to be heard. On the other side of the door the silence was being broken by the faint rise and fall of measured breathing just audible through the keyhole. A sliver of light on the threshold shone on the space where dust thickened; a flashlight was descending the frame from top to bottom. Not Mister King looking for his due; no, the movement was too deliberate, too cautious. Not the burglar I have been expecting either; that bastard when he comes will be more audacious, less hesitant. And I will have a hammer waiting for him. No, these sounds I knew best of all. Knew them all, all those years I heard them in my home; that anxious shuffle of feet was the same when as a child I had lain with my eyelids clamped shut; the nasal whistle was the same heard labour of custodial breathing outside the bedroom door when the evening was retreating and the skylight blackened overhead; the sudden artificial void of noise that amplified the silence was the sound of our common cowering.

Easy, easy.

Yes, it was my father, come at last.

SIX

I fled as soon as I could, escaping once I was sure the breathing outside had ceased and the torchlight would not return. There had been a knock on the door, and then another, a pause, and then another knock, and a longer pause after that, and then I had heard my father's feet retreating towards the steps that led to the street, and then on up the steps. I dared not twitch the curtains of the window, only waited until the blue-black of the night began to cede, for I could not bear to be apprehended and set upon in the dark. I dreaded the thought of being found among human and animal detritus, beaten and bruised, down an unforgiving lane, or else flung into the canal. I opened the door quietly and made my own way up the steps before turning onto Ivy Street, hurrying along next to the railings, feigning ignorance of the dim figure I sensed standing patiently, hand on belt, in the gloom of the half-opened black door. Instead I fixed my eyes on the pavement in front of me, resisting the urge to throw a glance in any other direction, to catch sight of who might be lurking there. Behind me I heard the familiar shlurp-tap shlurp-tapping of a gammy leg being dragged along the ground. I walked on with artificially brisk purpose, not so much to rouse his suspicions, but quickly enough to take advantage of his disability. I swore I could hear heavy panting, could smell his senescence on the breeze. The fool, I thought, had he not reckoned on my cunning? His mistake was to try and keep himself at a distance from me so as to go undetected, but had he not realised I was by now well practised in the arts of evasion? The old boy was not as nimble as I was, and not so sharp either, never had been, not with that defective leg. As soon as I reached the main road I lost him easily. A quick burst of speed and a leap onto the first bus that passed and I was out of reach. I threw a few of the mysterious coppers into the basket for the fare. I was glad I had them. Perhaps my luck was beginning to turn. The bus driver clicked his tongue and fired up the engine. It was then that I remembered that I had left behind what was left of the money – *my* money – in the flat and I cursed my forgetfulness. But there was no time for self-pity, for the bus had pulled off. From the window of the upper deck I craned my neck and looked out just to make sure that my father was clumping on up the road, all spidery-crooked legs and polished skull, his eyes haunted and fearful, a look of desperation on his face. But he was nowhere. On boy, let him go.

I knew without being fully conscious of it that I was on my way to the park. It came to me that perhaps my father would follow on the next bus so as soon as I arrived I hid in a ditch, skulking there among the brambles and weeds and used condoms and empty tin cans. I lurked there for several hours, feeling pleased that I had given him the slip, but wary, very wary still. Naturally, this feeling of satisfaction did not last because it was only a matter of time before my bum became wet from sitting on the mucky grass. Soon I would feel the damp seep into my groin. Once in a while the nearby hedges rustled and I started; my father, I thought, or maybe a bird or a rat, but in fact nothing came except for the odd flying insect, bees and wasps and dragonflies, and other things I did not know the names of. I watched a tiny-headed spider with oversized legs scramble over a moss-topped log, struggling to extract his inelegant legs from some sticky white sap, until eventually through sheer force of instinct he freed himself and disappeared stoically into the undergrowth to find, presumably, a mate or a meal. I stared up at the different formations of the clouds and played the children's game of finding faces there. I imagined I saw a neighbour I had once known, and Traudl, even myself, but it was all a lie really. They were just clouds, existing solely by themselves in whatever temporary shape they took, and whatever dim little meanings I found in them soon evaporated in air. Nothing else happened except that I farted twice or three times. After a while I got bored so I opened my trousers and tugged myself for a little while to see if I had completely dried up but in the circumstances I could conjure up nothing erotic and not even a pitiful dribble came out. I wiped myself on a leaf, but really there was no need, it was just for the sake of old habit. I was relieved to think that I might have been cured of the chronic urge to ejaculate at last. Now that I think about it, I realise I had been losing potency all along. Good.

When I was sure it was safe I wandered further into the forest, choosing paths I rarely chose, avoiding the busy benches scattered by the large lake, and avoiding especially the stone bridge and the pergola and the jetty. I went deep into the forest, and then deeper still. The old bastard would not find me now. He would struggle in the trees and would not be able to jump across the river that ran through the park. And so I settled myself down, not in a ditch, but in a clearing surrounded by birch trees on an island in the middle of a small lake in the middle of the forest.

Fitzgerald and I had known of the island from our childhood days when we would talk of building a raft and crossing the lake to live there by ourselves. But he was gone from me now. I waded resolutely through the waist-high water towards the green and mucky bank. If my bum was already wet, there was no use in complaining about my legs. The water was cold at first but soon I began to enjoy the numbing sensation. I had half-expected to cut my feet on the stones underneath, even prepared for the upwash of blood. I convinced myself leeches would attach to my skin, but the soft mud was unexpectedly pleasant and all I managed was to tread in a slippery cluster of warm, spotty jelly in the shallow waters of the island bank. Frogspawn, at this time of year? I should not have mentioned it at all. The alien leeches either. I pass on. Once out of the water and on the island I battled through the thick boles and pushed on towards the centre until I found what I was looking for: a grassy ring surrounded by trees, just as I had imagined it. Here in this perfect circle there was silence; here there was stillness. I wondered briefly if any of the branches would support the dead weight of a fully grown man. But I realised that I was not feeling as gloomy as I had the previous day. In fact, although the morning's pursuit had exhausted me and I had further ruined the clothes I had on me, I was buoyed by the victory I had achieved over my father. Vindicated, finally, even exhilarated. I pictured the old man, lugging his bad leg through the forest, up and down the pathways, crying out my name, seeking me out, hacking dramatically at the odd bush with a stick, until his cheeks puffed with tiredness and his heart pleaded for rest. Perhaps in such a weakened state I would have my chance to kill him, for once and for all, and bury him in the forest. The prospect of his death made me contemplative and elegiac. In the whirl of moods I was in I regretted that I had not brought writing things for my poetry, for I was building up quite a repository of usable tropes.

Barely breathing after all my exertions, I lay down on the grass for several hours, stretching out on the ground, gazing up at the sky through the encircling leaves. Gradually my heart stilled and calm descended. I took in the fresh air and rediscovered the freedom from the stench in my flat. I really don't know why I hadn't thought of it sooner, it seemed so simple. Time in the outdoors, that's what I needed, why hadn't I thought of that before? Live humbly, as one privileged creature among the innumerably privileged. Immerse myself in nature, let it anchor my authentic thoughts and guard my heart; that was the way to be free. Who said that? I forget. All this time I had been living in the stink when the fresh air was waiting for me to breathe it. I inhaled and exhaled deeply again, felt the cool breeze on the edge of my nostrils and visualised the flow of the air into my lungs. I unfurrowed my forehead and brought space between my eyebrows. A ray of sun burst through the branches and spread its warmth across my face. My skin tingled, no more, no less, no other sensation than that. I lay down on my back, took off my trousers, freed my genitals and stretched out my legs, the grass blades stirring in the cool breeze tickling my thighs and groin. The hair rose on my legs, no more than that. I did not suppress a smile.

I was surrounded by trees and water, and above me the sun, the stars, the moon, the wind, the clouds. Was this not plenty? So much else was eliminable. I could live off what I foraged, would that alone not be incentive enough? I felt my optimism growing. Were fish and berries no better or worse than the strict diet of porridge, raisins, bread and peas I had been on for the last few months? Food was surely abundant. How had I not noticed before all that nature had to offer? And what need had I now of money, the source of all my trouble? With money everything was transaction; but here on the island there was only symbiosis. I knew what I had to do. I reached into the pocket of my trousers, took out the few coppers I had been carrying all this time and threw them into the water. I was not able to account for them after all. They sliced through the last remaining clusters of the unseasonable frogspawn and were swallowed up, I presume, by the mud on the floor of the lake.

In the clean, unpolluted air thoughts were sudden and clear. I had interpreted Schorman's advice only partially. I had, I could see now, made a mistake. In my flat I had believed I would be alone, but I had been mistaken; everywhere I had been in the midst of others. No more intrusions, no more disruptions. Isolate, you must isolate. My mistake had been to believe that isolation involved a shrinking of the space instead of an enlargement of the world. Yes, I saw that now, truly saw it. No more would I be trapped in the city: how did I ever imagine that could I sever myself from its many beings, in living cheek by jowl with them? There, no matter where

I went, some new object was strewn in my path, pressing itself into my consciousness. If I stepped this way or that, the world was there, unimpeachably real, stretching along before me and behind me, giving all its many forms to me, unasked, un-answering, encumbering me with its multiple existences, and when I apprehended I was only one existing thing among countless others, something inside me began to turn, as if in my gut I felt the isolation I had sought was not actually possible but an unrealisable idea that had somehow been imposed upon me. In the city there were objects at every hand's turn: parked cars and scattered lampposts, skeletal bicycle wheels chained to railings, their tyres now saggy rubber corpses, the frames long-since departed. Dog turds were carelessly deposited here and there on the pavement. I say carelessly, but how was I to know? Perhaps they had been left there with some vague purpose in mind? Perhaps the owner of the dog had... but I do not know the answer to these meaningless questions! The drying remains of some recently ejected phlegm formed a grubby puddle to the human and a treacherous, sticky pond to the insect. And then my childhood landscapes, all around, the half-hearted trappings of suburban disguise: electricity boxes painted in that dark, unconvincing green, stray car-tracks slashing kerbside rectangles of yellowy grass, all those mis-placed trees and bushes and flowers fighting dumbly for a life they could not help but have in a place of human choosing. This is to say nothing of the people intruding in on each other as they moved about the streets in individual purpose, breathing in each other's gases, and all the cold buildings they had erected to obscure the horizon. Everywhere I looked were things and the remnants of things stamping their fractious existences on the street, their destinies only now manifest as the once-had-been or never-was. I had secreted myself away in the flat in an effort to hide myself away from these things, but now I saw my mistake: would not simplicity and isolation best be found not in my concrete and plywood bolthole, but instead in the limitless open of the countryside? I saw now that I had been seeking a world by generating it solely out of myself; that had been my cardinal error.

I pictured myself leaving the island and setting up in a cosy, converted stable, a stone haven in an old courtyard in the middle of empty fields, spending my days in silent reflection, with only the chirping of finches and tits for company. But why stop there, why should I settle at all in a house, why lock myself up in brick and glass and wood, the house was a mistake for Christ's sake, an habitual error, why do I not learn that, why can I never see that, why not keep moving, keep burning, why not go to those treeless mountains that sweep down to the sea, further on into those mountains I had rambled over from the time I was a boy, when I was sensitive, curious, diffident, past Cruagh Wood and the Pine Forest, past the dilapidated colonial country estates, and further on up Montpellier Hill, up and further up the steepening slopes, rising up above the rising noises of my childhood, live shelterless there, my eyes turned toward the sea, roaming over the city, my puny body exposed to the pouring rays of the sun, and the chilling rain that would surely follow, apprehending my naked existence, plumbing the darkest abyss, communing with nature uninterrupted, pursuing the question into the black night, where at last the vast, infinite universe would render up its glittering secrets to me? There I would not be distanced from the eternal truths, but de-severed and brought closer to them in one last effort. I had been an oversized presence in a tiny place, but to be a tiny speck in the immense cosmos, that's the way to be free. Freedom, I cried, freedom! But stop! Stop. Breathe. I was letting my imagination run away with me again. I am not ready for immeasurable, inhuman space, for the perpetual presence of the sublime.

That day, as the hours passed, I watched the clear, blue sky spread into a comforting vermillion glow. It happened slowly, so slowly I barely noticed it happen at all, just a gradual incarnadining of the earlier light, until I sensed that the colour of everything around me had been adjusted, and then it all turned a deeper shade, as if my descrying of the scene had left the birch trunks wearing blushes. I lay there breathing until the evening light soon began to splinter down through the trees, throwing orange and pink spears around my body. I watched the pond skaters on the lake surface for a while. An otter snuck out of some bankside scrub and slid into the water. A warm, gentle breeze was blowing. An approximate happiness. I closed my eyes and inhaled deeply, filling my lungs, sending sweet, cool air down into my belly. The evening was turning to twilight and the birds were beginning to jostle for the best perches, letting out the occasional squeal as they found their place in the hierarchy. Bats flitted. A hedgehog snuffled. Trees soughed. To tell the truth, I was not altogether entirely happy about the activity around me. Impossible not to reach out beyond myself. Things were infiltrating through the senses. My peace was being assailed by small intrusions and though I

107

tried to empty my mind, I could feel my thoughts pouring out and conferring meaning on any sound I heard or movement that caught my eye.

I closed my eyes again to shut out the world, but then I was alone with myself and the images that arose before me were no less intrusive. My mother there, book resting on lap, neck snapped back and head to the ceiling, curled purple lips, teeth bared. Traudl too, swollen nipples prodding through her dress, the creature writhing, bellyskin rippling. Before long the masturbatory urge started up too. So, wrong again. There is no respite from its implacable demand. I was at least heartened by the absence of stimuli, at least in human terms; I knew the island was flush full of natural commotion, and even though two spiders were mating on a dropped branch beside me, the sexual feeling soon wore off and I returned to my usual flaccid state, much to my relief, however temporary.

In any event I was mistaken about the mating spiders: in fact it was a fight to the death. They reminded me of something, those hate-filled spiders, the entangled legs, the sharp pine needles on which they enacted their embroilment, the deathly embrace. The victor appeared to eat its victim, but I couldn't be certain, everything was so minute. This reminded me too that I was hungry and I heard a rumbling in my belly, right on cue. I realised that I had not eaten since the previous day. I looked around me but I couldn't find any of the berries I had intended to live off. A form of immediate sustenance presented itself as a troop of ants crawling over my legs. Protein, iron. Inspired, I smashed my palms on my trousers and licked the smudge of their remains. I had expected the ants to taste sour but they tasted only what I imagine dirt to taste of, with a slight metallic hint that was not disagreeable. It was really only a matter of getting used to the texture of tiny, hairy legs and antennae. Admittedly, I was not entirely satisfied by the ants but my appetite was not what it once was. Once I had eaten as many ants as I could stomach and drank my fill from the lake, I found a nearby bush and settled myself down to sleep. The water was a dun colour and tasted a little stagnant, and though I nearly vomited several times I kept it down in the end.

The warmth of the day was beginning to depart, and the stars were coming out. I lay down on the ground and scanned the night sky for the horns of Taurus. The giant, tangerine Aldebaran was there too; the Seven Sisters just beyond. My lids grew heavy with the searching. I did not fight the sleep when it came.

Woken by the snap of a branch. My father? (He had hunted me out before – once, I ran away from home when I was a teenager. I wandered the streets of our suburb until I came to settle in the doorway of the local church; at last the headlights of his car turned full glare on me and he stepped out into the night. I knew I would get a sound beating for my attempted flight, and so I did.) Had he found my island? I armed myself with a small log, tensed my paltry muscles and steeled myself for an attack. Nothing appeared, but that was no confirmation that there was nothing there. Something was stuck between my teeth but I dared not pick at it. More rustling in the bushes by my side. Perhaps it was a bird dropping off its perch, I thought. Perhaps – but perhaps nothing. I couldn't see very well in spite of the fact that the stars were gleaming overhead and a bright, full moon was shining. The bark of the birch trees glistened and silver beams lasered onto the floor of the clearing. Yet everywhere too there were dense black patches through which I could not see; the bushes were vague, shadowy forms at best. In the light and the half-light and the darkness I was confused. It seemed as if an obscure form was moving nearby, dimly, through the trees, feeling its way through the branches. I convinced myself I heard breathing so I slowed my own down until I became giddy and nearly passed out. The air was sharp and cold on my nostrils. I held the log over my head, ready to crack the head of the intruder. But no, there was no more sound. I must have peered into the darkness to see again that shadowy figure for more than an hour but nothing or no one appeared. Emboldened, I scrabbled in the undergrowth for the bird but found nothing. I accidentally put my hand in a slime-like substance, the precise nature of which I cannot say. I know what it was, but I can't say it.

It wasn't long before it started to pour with rain. My goose-pimpled arms were shivering and my elbows started to flex and rise involuntarily, lifting up towards my chin and resting down in a crossed position on my chest as in the fashion of the dead. Short, spikey exhalations escaped from my lungs. My hair was cold and water was dripping down my nose, and I soon developed an icy sweat. Something was swelling on my left ankle and the entire foot itched from the dampness of the sock; my right foot was cramping in its shoe, which felt as if it had shrunk. I realised every part of me was sodden and I soon began to feel sick in my stomach. I retched once or twice but nothing came out, just a dribble of spit which clung stubbornly to my beard and which I couldn't reach with my tongue. Above me the moon was obscured, clouded over now, and the stars were only a memory. I studied the sky to see what hour it was but time meant nothing to me, it was neither moving slowly nor quickly; for all I could tell it was neither night nor day, but an eternal, dark grey. Nor did I care, for there was a new actuality: a rapacious craving for food that was intensifying by the minute.

As the hunger grew I could not help but think about it, and the more I thought about it the worse it got. Then as I got used to it there were bouts where I ended up staring upward at the falling rain, completely absent from myself, almost in bliss, as if it were simply an unignorable but manageable embarrassment. In those moments I would nearly lose myself but then I would be brought back to consciousness by the gnawing in my gut, and I would realise that nothing was as true as physical pain. Now I was so hungry I started to hanker after anything, even after, yes, even after some more ants. I discovered pain had its virtues. Although I was almost entirely consumed by hunger, there were moments of clarity that without it would not have been possible. The agony in my stomach, for instance, made a fool of my fabled will. There was no such thing as freedom for living beings; there never had been, that was all a pack of lies, for freedom would simply mean the end of the tyranny of the body and all its degrading cravings, and that freedom would simply be the negation of life itself. I saw all that now. In fact that's another lie. I had known it all along but I had forgotten it, no, that's not true either, I had made myself forget. You will say that makes no sense. Forget I said anything. Now I was being humiliated by the cold and merciless truth of this appetite. But more than that, hunger itself was eating my innards.

The day passed and my stomach pains were so bad that I took to chewing moss off a branch, which I promptly vomited up. A warm drizzle fell for hours. I started sweating again, perspiration dripping down into my eyes and over my lips and into my mouth. I opened my mouth to drink the rain, and tried again swallowing my spit over and over, now salty from the sweat, but it only made my mouth thirst for more as it had before. Then I did it again. I thought of my flat, and all that I had left behind, my bread and porridge and peas, but I couldn't keep my concentration, and I ended up just staring into space as the seconds and minutes beat out every moment and the closing in of my death. I tore off a piece of the leather from my left shoe and chewed on it, seeing nothing, watching nothing, getting no nutrition, nothing. I saw a squirrel halfway up the tree, nibbling on a nut, and decided immediately to catch, kill and eat it. Ordinarily, I would have congratulated myself for such decisiveness, but the mere fact that this disgusting creature was eating in front of me was reason enough for its destruction. Emboldened by the thought of fresh meat, I pressed myself up from the ground, my clothes sticky and tight and uncomfortable, coming apart now at the seams, the sole of the shoe on my right foot had come completely loose and my toe was sticking out from it, but I stealthily crept up as best I could on the squirrel with murderous intent. I stepped ever so slowly towards it, taking care not to tread on any sticks, taking up a position behind a nearby bush. My movement must have alerted it. The squirrel stopped nibbling and fixed a wary eye on me. I stood utterly still, winning momentarily the fight with the severe pain in my belly, which was really a fight with myself, autosacrophagous parasite that I was. The squirrel was taunting me. Where had it found those delicious nuts? I had searched and searched but could find no tree bearing nuts. The animal resumed its meal. I dared not breathe. The squirrel turned its eyes away from me. Suddenly, when I judged the moment to be right, I leapt out from the bush towards the creature with my hands outstretched, believing I could get enough height and catch it before it would realise what was happening and had the opportunity to scurry away. My plan was to hold it by the tail and swing it against the tree with my last remaining strength until I had dashed its brains out. But in my haste I slipped in some slime, stubbed the exposed toe on a rock, and then my knee came flying up in a reflex and smashed into my chin, loosening a tooth in the process. I lost my balance and banged my head against the trunk of the tree. I felt a new wave of pain gush through me and I slumped down, my head badly grazed, blood streaming down my face and in my mouth, my toe and chin aching. At least it distracted momentarily from the hunger. I swallowed the blood too. I looked up and saw the squirrel sitting ignorantly on a branch overhead and then felt a small bump as the nutshell it had discarded landed on my brow. I put the shell into my mouth, grateful at least for this fortune, but it was inedible and I soon retched it up again, my loose tooth coming out with the force of the heaving.

*　　　*　　　*

As the hours passed I discovered that it was I who was the food. There were creatures that came out at the close of day: mosquitoes and midges and horseflies that bit me and drank my blood. I clawed at them frantically in the descending dusk and smashed them as I had the ants between my hands until my palms were stained red and black, licking the remains for whatever nourishment I could get, but I could not kill them all and ignorant of my brute power they feasted on me with insectival apathy. My eyes kept closing over and I eventually fell asleep. A badger – on an island? – must have mistaken my body for a corpse and gnawed at my hands and feet until I woke with a start and clobbered it with my log. And if they could not get at my flesh, there were creatures that ate my clothes: it was not long before mice came and nibbled at my shoelaces and the collar of my shirt, even a pygmy shrew that ate the slugs that had crawled up onto my crotch. I thought of Traudl, my Traudl, and the creature in her womb, devouring her from the inside out, and my eyes began to itch. And where was my father, he who had thrown me into this world and then persecuted me for attention? Why had he not come for me? He was responsible for all this; it was he who had forced this torment upon me. Quivering with a strange enervated rage, I shouted into the trees, *Where are you father?* I walked to the bank of the island and called his name again, just to test his presence.

Father, father, here I am, I cried. *Father, where are you?*

Then I shouted a vile word, and an even viler one, I even got a little excited, so I shouted some more, the shouting relieved me, worked myself up a little but there was no reply and I was soon exhausted from all the shouting. No sound, no soul. Utterly myself. The immense night star-strewn sky, the constellations silently circling in the heavens above me. So this is what it was to finally be alone. I shrank back into the trees, willing myself to believe that the feeling I had that mine was an existence by proxy was a just product of my hunger, with only the unbearable ache reproving my doubt.

Dawn came with birdsong, first one, then two, then three, and then all of them in a great dissonant choir. The pangs worsened. To distract myself, I tried to pick out the species. Was that a thrush, or a lark? In some field in the park birdwatchers would be listening in open-eared joy, jotting down the times and sounds in their little blue-lined copybooks. But they were voluntary auditors whereas I could not help but hear. The more I heard, the less I wanted to hear. I blocked my ears, but eventually more and more birds joined in until the trees came fully alive with competitive squawking. Krrrrk. Krrrrrrrrk. Krrrwwwwwwwk. Fury was surging up inside me and the proper source of this fury was this hateful esurience that insisted upon itself and was turning everything in nature into my enemy, including myself, for what was I but one of nature's own? I went in search of something for breakfast, anything, I even considered the grass, recalling from my school books the illustrations of food-crazed famine victims, dumped in the ditches with dark green smears on their hands and mouths. The grotesque absurdity of the comparison made me giddy with laughter. I plunged my hand into the lake to tickle a fish but they all swam away from me with what seemed like easy, comical disdain. Blundering about the trees, I finally came across a tall one full of nuts – the source of my squirrel's meal yesterday no doubt – but they were all on the highest branches and there were none that I could reach. I laughed cynically. By now I was truly starving and starting to hallucinate. I cursed myself and shouted insults, directing them at my oversized clown-feet in particular, they were a disgrace, had always been a disgrace. Look at those revolting bunions, horrible calloused embarrassments. How could I walk around with those feet, had I no shame? My disgusting feet called attention to the rest of me. For the first time in a long time I observed my clothes, which had now become torn and ragged. I looked into the lake water. My lip was all swollen from the injury I had done to my mouth and there was dried blood on my chin. I gurned. The missing tooth was a red-black space in my mouth. There were scrapes all over my forehead where I had cut myself on branches and twigs. Good. After all I was starting to look the part, finally. The birds kept squawking, interrupting my miserable self-reflections. I looked up at them. Some of them were wheeling about overhead, but most of them sat in the branches. I flung a stone blindly into the trees, and then another stone, and another, but nothing struck and on and on went the horrible screeching that rang in my ears now like callous, avian laughter. The trees were calling to me now, *hang, hang, hang,* my true animal state finally revealed to me by this hunger, but at the thought of another pathetic melodrama, I heard my cackles echo against the hollows of the trees.

I could stand it no longer. A short time later, my gut screwed up with the pangs, I abandoned my island. Using up the last of my energy, I slid into the lake and waded back to the mainland, implausible leech offspring nursing on my blood.

*   *   *

I spent the day skulking down an alleyway off Camden Street, scavenging bits of thrown-away sandwiches and fruit and crisps, anything I could find to kill my hunger, waiting for night to fall once more. The moon rose. It was time to go. I slunk through the dim streets, doing my best to avoid all human contact, but it was no use, for he was still there, my beggar friend, turning pages, mouthing the words of a language I did not know. As I passed him, he caught my stare and shrank back into the gloom, his eyes glinting with mischief and caution. I treaded slowly, the better to hear the sound of other footsteps on the cold, damp concrete, the better to disguise my own movements. In and out of the shadows I weaved, avoiding the glare of the lamplight, using the many objects on the street, cars and walls, postboxes and electricity poles, to hide myself. Eventually I reached the building on Ivy Street, for I had nowhere else to go, and besides I needed my money. All the curtains were drawn. The black door was shut. I held my breath and descended the concrete steps in the corner of the building to the basement level. I crouched as I passed by the window, taking care to avoid the mush of leaves on the ground. My foot brushed against a flower pot but my reflexes were quick and I steadied it before it fell over. A sudden metallic crashing was the sound of a fox turning over a bin lid nearby, but I held my nerve. I knelt down and fingered the letter box, grateful that I had oiled the hinges, and I peered inside. It was too dark to see, but nothing seemed to be moving. I pressed my ear to the door but could not hear a sound. Good. Making progress. I turned the key in the lock and pushed the door, which I noticed had been painted an unfamiliar dark blue. A new smell was hanging in the air but now, for Christ's sake, get on with it, now was not the moment to succumb to my sensitivities. On with it boy. Steeling myself for what lay ahead of me, I clenched my fists, ready for violence, ready for murder, and flicked on the light. I scuttled about the room swinging my arms in riotous windmills and shouting obscenities and trying not to breathe, like a madman I suppose you might say, if that's what you want to say, I even got a little excited, but it was not long before I saw my wild gestures were pointless in the personless and silent room and I soon calmed down.

On the table were strewn papers and writing things that were not my own, of which there was no sign. The papers were mostly official-looking documents, headed letters, franked envelopes. The presence of another here, supplanting me, as if I had never existed. Virginia's bowl too was gone, and in its place was a little yellow canary in a bell-shaped birdcage. There were large books in old blue and brown leather deposited here and there, crowding up the once-empty spaces on the shelves. I noticed the flat had been newly coated a deep, luxurious shade of red. A pair of black trousers with impossibly long legs were draped over the back of a purple velvet armchair. The door to the bedroom was ajar but though I was curious about the new burgundy carpet that had been laid I had not the courage to look inside its dark interior. The bird started screeching noisily so I opened the cage to do what, I don't know, to shut it up or to let it out. It escaped immediately, furiously bashing its wings on the metal wires in its haste, before flying out through the door to the flat which I had forgotten to close behind me. I could not delay long. The plush colours were becoming oppressive. I ran immediately to the press in the kitchen to find the envelope of money that I had left behind me in the margarine tub, taking note of the sharp knife skewered in a loaf of bread, which I promptly devoured. Though I had been gone for some days, the envelope, which I stuffed in my pocket, was still there, and I allowed myself a brief self-congratulatory smile at the effectiveness of my cunning.

The stink of fresh varnish was beginning to suffocate my throat and hurt my head. No sound coming from outside. I cocked my ear to the ceiling. Silence too from the upstairs. I went back out onto the street, taking in gulps of fresh air. The recent wet weather had chipped off some more of the paintwork on the façade of the building. I cast my eyes upwards to the three windows on the first floor. The same lace curtains and rotting frames as before. I knew where I was going to go, as if it had all been preordained. I crossed over the three worn-away steps that formed the little bridge over the basement level to the black door. I leaned against it, expecting it to be locked, but to my surprise it swung open. A door on the right and the left, and a staircase halfway down the corridor. The air was cold and smelled of damp. A strange humming noise was coming from somewhere, the source of which I could not identify. Thick dust wafted in the air. I choked a little but pressed on. Ignoring the two doors, which I knew would be locked anyway, I went upstairs. At the top of the flight was another single door. I put my eye to the keyhole, swivelling my eyeballs this way and that, but could see nothing nor nobody inside. I rolled the old round knob. A new, cold object in my hand that felt alien and unwieldy, for a moment my gut began to surge. When I heard the click of the lock sliding back, I released the door from its jamb and entered the upstairs flat.

It was twice as large as the flat in the basement, and I was immediately disorientated by the space. Yet it also contained only the fundamentals, more or less, as my flat had before: a chair, a table, a desk, a bed, a mirror, a stove, even a hammer under the sink, a press – stop. You know the rest. Among these familiar objects I felt at ease. And here was space; here was room enough. What need had I of anything larger? Simplify, isolate. No more of that; I haven't the heart any more. It had not been repainted, as far as I could tell, as before. I went to one of the side windows and looked through the curtains, taking care not to twitch them. Deserted things on the street, inert, unobserving, full bins and bent bicycle wheels and strewn cars, bits of wrappers and other untold entities. But no people, not anywhere. Alone at last. I caught sight of myself in the mirror and barely recognised the person before me; my clothes and shoes were ragged and ripped, my face and hands scabrous and filthy, pinched at the cheekbones, gaunt and brittle. I had lost some hair on the front of my head, though it was sprouting in my ears and nose. Staring deep into the mirror I inspected my eyes, shrunken back into protruding sockets and bloodshot.

It occurred to me that I had not seen my body in weeks. I took off all my clothes, peeling away the last remaining bloodied and sweated rags that had stuck to my skin, my shirt, the remains of my trousers, my socks and shoes. My underpants were crusted and stained where I had soiled myself. They were clinging to the perineum, and I had to tear them away from the skin. It had never been much use to me as an erogenous zone in any case, for all the feathering I had done there. Let it bleed. I was sorry I had not thought of skinning myself there before. There I was, finally, naked before myself. I was making progress, finally. Gossamerskin threadbare over peninsular ribs. Bones jutting out into the emptiness about me. Lower belly distended and patched with brown moss. Arms and legs like autumnal twigs. I barely recognised myself, yes, but recognised in that ignorance the aging self behind it that was somewhere between life and death. For this degenerate body I was housed within was me and was not me, the remnant flesh of that which I had been and which I now was, a living offcut of the past.

In the corner of the flat was a wardrobe, where I found a navy suit and white shirt in a dry-cleaner's plastic wrapping. I unwrapped the clothes and put them on, and looked at myself in the mirror, twirling this way and that, grinning and pouting, just to, I don't know, to amuse myself. The suit did not fit me badly, in fact, I thought, might even have been tailored for me. There was nothing I could do about my missing tooth, but in the circumstances I was glad to be in fresh clothes, which were, I admit, growing on me by the minute. I went to the window and looked out. No movement outside. I was feeling hungry again, so I rummaged in the bin. Underneath the mouldy slices of bread and old, black potato peelings, which I ate anyway, were some pages. I reached down and pulled them out. I read the first one to hand, a ripped fragment covered in a cream stain:

Does death come into the world through being undone by the experience of grief for the deaths of others, or can the limitations of mortality only be grasped in relation to the inexorable yet inexperienceable event of one's own death? And is the case that death is a contingent, mysterious fact or is it the single destination on the infinite horizons on which we hurl our lived experiences and the ultimate destiny that drives meaning into all potentialities?

I reached further into the bin, retrieving more and more pages, and there too, under all these pages, were more pages still, and fragments of pages and more stained pages, and underneath all those pages were poems and books too, philosophies, fictions and sciences. I emptied the bin on the floor, pouring all the pages and books on the ground. I pulled the chair over to the table, and one by one, began to sort and pile, sort and pile. When I had finished, I placed the books on some empty shelves. I took one down and began to leaf through it, gliding a finger over the words, mouthing their sounds, absorbing into my brain the ideas they contained. Something was stirring inside me again. Among the blackened pages on the floor were white ones. They were calling to me, almost willing me to blacken them. I picked up the whole lot and a pen dropped out, nib first, coming to rest beside my hand. So here I was. I jotted down a sentence and read it out aloud, testing my voice. It wobbled a little, so I spoke it again, this time carefully emphasising each syllable. I stood up and sat down again, then stood up and went to the window. Nobody there. I looked behind me. A blank page gleamed on the table. Unformed thoughts were forming.

I was not unhappy.

Nightly I press my ear to the door, or glance out of the window at the shadowy parts of the street. Nobody comes. Page by page, chapter by chapter, the document is growing, filling up the space on my table, a testament to my existence. Summer turns to autumn and the evenings are a beautiful warm orange glow. I watch the sun setting over the red rooftops as full-throated birds perched along the telephone wires outside the window chirped happily. Careful. At night-time I move my chair over to the window and pick out the constellations as they slowly wheel through the sky. Gauzed by the curtains and the street lights they are less distinct, and I drop a star here and there, but I can still make them out or where they should be; Polaris, of course, but Cepheus too, and the great square of Pegasus. Silence too from the downstairs.

SEVEN

Something was beginning to stink, and I feared the knock on the door, knew it would be coming, every day bringing closer the moment those outstretched bony fingers will collar me. Time running out. Space shrinking. Now I worked on the question, resolute, determined, making progress, thinking harder and harder still until the images and ideas became hardened in my head, this was the present, this was my life, and one day, when I could think no more, harden the images and ideas no more, I sent my papers to Schorman for the final arbitration. *That's it*, I cried, *I have it now!* I pictured him, sitting at his desk, engrossed in my prose, his joy brimming over as I entered the room. He rises to embrace me, brotherly, affectionately, lovingly. *Oh my boy, oh my boy! Such resplendent reasoning, such wonderful erudition of this most complex phenomenological issue.* I could feel my crotch dampen. To distract myself I opened a can of tuna. I remembered fondly the ants. I eyed the raw peppers I had stolen in a rebellious fit the previous day and promised I would have them for a treat when I returned. I became restless. I set off, a little impulsively, yes, down to the university to see him. At the corner of Ivy Street I came across my beggar friend, sitting there reading, reading what, it doesn't matter what he was reading, call it *Sult*, will that do, fingering the words on the page, smirking to himself. I should have embraced him, my friend in misery, but as he had his back turned to me I spat on his neck, I don't know why, don't ask me why, I just felt like it, is that not enough? I shouted an insult at him and ran away before he could catch me. I sniggered to myself, the bastard. It was a warm day. A gentle breeze was blowing. I was not unhappy.

I reached the university and headed for Schorman's office. By the time I had arrived I was feeling optimistic. I pushed open the door in a hurry and threw myself into the room, closing the door quietly but firmly behind me, announcing myself to him. Schorman stood up and grabbed a pen to defend himself against his would-be assailant, his eyes in wide surprise.

You, he said, recognising me at last and lowering the pen, *I was not expecting you. Don't you ever knock?*

He was wearing a tight white shirt. Some chest hair was poking through the gaps between the buttons. Later I would run a hand over my own chest to feel my own hair, discretely, when I was sure no one was looking, drawing circles around my nipples and making them erect.

Well, he said, *what is the meaning of this intrusion?*

Professor Schorman, I would be very grateful if you could see me at such short notice, I said, a little breathlessly. *You may have seen that I sent you some work. I believe I have made some progress on the question...*

Lock that door, said Schorman suspiciously, *I will have no more interruptions. This is a private space.* He eyed me. *I fear I have made a very bad error of judgment with you.*

Profess... I began apologetically.

He cocked his head to one side and regarded me intently.

Quiet now. Shh. Fingers to his lips. Eyes to the side of his head. *Listen! Do you hear anything? Do you?*

I listened intently. Nothing.

Schorman's eyes fell on my pages, running his fingers through his hair and pushing his large chest out. I sat on the plastic chair and began fiddling with the fronds of the rubber plant. A hmm. A click. A hmm. A click.

These pages of yours, resumed Schorman after a while, *yes, I saw them. I tried reading them but your handwriting is illegible. Have you still no computer for god's sake? In any event I cannot get to the ground of your question. This document you have sent me. Is it... what is the word... a parergon?*

Not quite, I said. *The work is not yet complete, but I feel that I am coming close to the end.*

Ssh! Again! Do you hear that? asked Schorman again, looking up at me, the finger to his lips again. Schorman shook his head. I could see he was moved by something approximating pity. *Total silence. Endless silence.* Schorman's voice grew softer. *The Head of Department. Last week. No more tapping. It just stopped. No more tapping. No more poems. When I think of the work he produced. We were very proud of him in the university, you know, he was a great asset to us*, he said plaintively. *Now, not even poetry.*

Very bold ideas he had, Schorman went on. He leafed absent-mindedly through my pages. *Very bold. The era of contingency was over, he had argued. A new species of man needed to appear, he said, one whose destiny lay in truth. A man of conviction. A man of credibility. A man of substance...*

A man of substance? I interjected.

Indeed, said Schorman. *A man of substance.*

Schorman sat back in his chair, gazing into the middle distance. Outside the roses were in bloom, their heads swaying this way and that in the haphazard air. The gardener sauntered along, cutting the grass, the low, persistent buzz of the blade forcing its diminished drone against the glass. Past the window he came and then went out of sight.

He was a very bold and great thinker, Schorman continued. He spoke as if I was not there. *He was convinced in his ideas. In the cafés in the morning, in the streets at midday, in the pubs at night, he set about converting those who would not believe. In restaurants, to the embarrassment of his companions, he raised his voice so those near him could hear. When they crowded away from him, he spoke more loudly. He even*, and here Schorman lowered his voice to a whisper, *made love to a female colleague so that he could beseech her in her most vulnerable state. Yet, he was met with indifference and befuddlement, silence, even contempt. They fondly mocked him, like a halfwit brother, but that fondness turned to derision. They asked for detail. He said that detail obscured the truth. They asked for truth. He said that truth was only a question. They asked for answers. He said that answers were only proof of questions. They began asking for proof. He said that proof was in the detail.*

What he really wanted, Schorman explained, suddenly turning his attention to me, *was mutuality and dialogue. This courage was due to his fundamental honesty.*

Is that right? I asked.

Schorman held up his hand at me to be quiet.

He never lied. They said terrible things. Terrible things! He was a pervert, a deviant, a factotum for an irrepressible and well known homosexual. Another said no, that it was he who had encouraged homosexuality in an impressionable lover. His sex life was the subject of relentless gossip. It was ludicrous to call him a homosexual, others said, when he was an inveterate fucker of women. Yes, Schorman told me, getting a little excited, *they said he had deliberately impregnated a student to prove a scientific theory and then forced her to have an abortion to prove a political point. Others said on the contrary she had carried out the abortion to punish him financially but her plan backfired. He was not so wealthy as she had imagined, and he had to use part of the State grant he received for an ambitious research project to pay for the termination. But even still, she had paid the most. Oh there were other slanders, terrible things said about him,* Schorman said, looking out the window, shaking his head from side to side, picking some fluff off his shirt. His eyes moistened. For a moment I feared he would cry.

Such a beautiful man. You should read the poems he has written: such insight.

My eyes fell on Schorman's chest, rising now with the ever-increasing rapidity of his speech. He grew more excited as he spoke, breathless now as he recanted the tale.

Are you listening to me? Schorman asked, fixing his intense eyes on me.

Go on, I said.

They accused him of sophistry and stupidity, of hiding behind rhetoric and of yet being hidden by words. One night in the pub, the ringleader of his tormentors, a prolific writer to the letters pages of the newspapers, called him a fucking blackguard and threatened to cut his throat if he would not retract. There was no such thing as truth, they said, *was he going to perpetuate a lie?* Schorman's voice had been rising in volume all this time. I could see he was by now highly agitated. He banged his fists against the table, sending papers flying to the ground.

A man of substance! he shouted. *Is that how a man of substance is to be treated?*

There was a moment's silence. I dared not shuffle my feet. I realised by the fierceness of his gaze that Schorman was directing the question at me. I did not know the answer to this question and shrugged my shoulders, helplessly.

Well? Is it? Schorman demanded again.

I don't know, I said.

He shook his head.

No. You don't. How could you?

I did not know what to say. *Professor Schorman...*

Do you know what it is to love another? Do you? I could see his lip was wobbling now, and his eyes were filling with tears.

The document, Professor Schorman, have you read it?

There was a moment's silence. Then Schorman's face turned bright red and his arms shook. For a moment I thought he would attack me. I coiled my fists in my pockets and tightened the muscles in my stomach.

Don't you see anything? Don't you understand anything at all? I am wasting my time with you. My life – my life – is draining away, second by second, and I am being forced to read these mindless, rambling pages of yours, forced to listen to your words. They go nowhere. My life is slipping away and you are not concerned!

He slumped back into his chair and waved his hand dismissively in my direction. No one spoke. The silence was broken by the drifting sound of keys once more being tapped.

Have you isolated yourself as I suggested? Schorman asked me wearily.

I have tried.

And yet it seems to me that if you have, then you have not understood. I think you are lying to me. Have you been lying to me all along? Have you been making up stories? The last I heard from you I recall there was some nonsense about a dead mother and a suicidal friend and some stolen money. Arising now from his chair. Navigating the corner of his desk. *Have you been making up stories? Lying to me?* Sitting in front of me and leaning forward, his face was so close that I could smell his sweet, confectionary smell. Schorman grabbed me by my shirt; some of my chest hair got caught in his grip and my nipples became sore. I had an urge to lick his face, to taste the salty sweat on his brow and feel his warm breath on my face.

He let go of me and I slid back in my chair.

Your question, he sighed after a moment. *Well then. Let's go over what I take to be the substance of your work. Look out the window there and tell me what you see.*

Relieved, I saw a familiar figure. *I see the gardener on a mower, passing by the window again.*

Is he a real man?

Yes.

How do you know that?

131

He is unmistakably a man. He is wearing his overalls and his cap. I could say that he may well be a ghost in clothes, or that he is a robot being moved about by some unseen controls, but I still say that he is a conscious man acting freely and I believe what I see with my own eyes.

Where does this belief lie?

It lies within my own mind. It cannot lie anywhere else.

And there can be no uncertainty about that.

None. Belief is not external to the human mind. I see a man on a mower. I see no reason to disbelieve. I see a man on his mower. That is what I believe to be the truth.

Schorman turned to face the window. He clicked his tongue in his cheek and said, *So, he is a man, and you believe this because this is your perception. Listen now. You have taken a single aspect of your experience of reality and made it an absolute truth. How have you established this truth? You believe that the answer to questions can irrefutably be found by recourse to the testimony of your own eyes and the rest of your senses. Naturally, what you want is deliverance from contingency. But in doing so, you have subjected everything outside this truth to a kind of terror. You remake reality in your own fashion, but in doing so you have destroyed the natural relationship you have with the world. This relationship is not a matter of faith, or belief, or perception. Don't you see?* He waved my pages at me. *You speak as if some strange thing has entered you,* he said, *but you are in life as if you are in the element to which you have the most affinity. Like a blind fish,* he added, *in the deepest trench of the ocean.*

Schorman lit up a cigarette and eyed me through the rising smoke. He pulled deep on the fag, his pupils dilating.

You have a disordered way of thinking. Your task, he said, *is not to create the world, or imagine it, or to find it, as if it were alien to you. Your task is to live in it. To inhabit it.* His voice wobbled pathetically. *To love within it. To die within it.*

I thought with horror that tears would fall but he did not blink. On the whole I was grateful. But my early morning enthusiasm had waned once more. I felt self-conscious under his stare so I watched a spider climb into a corner where the walls and ceiling met, and settle there, waiting.

There is a disgusting smell coming from you, do you know that? Schorman said, sniffing the air with obvious distaste. He did not conceal his disgust.

The spider hung perfectly still in the corner through some imperceptible force.

Tell me, Schorman asked brusquely, opening the window, *How did it end for your friend, the one you were worried about?*

Fitzgerald? Not well, I said.

No?

No. Someone told me a jogger found him swinging from a tree.

Schorman looked out the window. The gardener had gone, the buzz of his mower fading.

I see, he said. *Then it's all over for him.*

Yes, I said.

I see. You have a lot of work to do yet. I do not want to see you again until the document is completed. There is nothing I can help you with right now, you have not understood, he said slowly. *You need to begin again.*

Schorman sat back down on his chair and slung one leg

over the other. He rested his elbow on his knee, propped his chin and cheek in his hand and slowly closed his eyes. Then he thought hard about how a man might live and die in this world.

*　　　*　　　*

A week or two have passed since my visit to Schorman. One day as I was wandering by the canal I spied an old plastic clock in a rubbish bin. I fished it out and brought it home and was pleased to find it was still working. Round and round the hands went, circling the stationary numbers. When I woke from sleep and dreams, the clock was the first thing I looked at.

This new possession has become important to me. From the moment I hung it on the bedroom wall, though I have sometimes pretended otherwise, I knew that I would be conscious of its movements, alert always to its pococurante tick-tock.

*　　　*　　　*

All was not lost. There was another, the only other. I did a calculation. The baby would be nearing its birth. Traudl would save me, had only ever saved me. I dialled her number. It rang and rang until it ceased. I dialled again, and let it ring, until eventually Cullen answered.

Traudl, I said, *Traudl?*

Cullen's voice cracked as he started to speak. He coughed and hocked, clearing his throat. Traudl wasn't able to talk right now, he told me, she was still in the hospital. *The baby*, he started before drifting off. *The baby?* I asked. He did not speak. Then all at once he starting jabbering, pouring words down the line like water over the edge of an overflowing bath. It was too late. It had been a difficult birth. There was confusion over the procedure and the midwife had been less than skilled, although it didn't matter in the end. In the end the baby had been born, the outcome assured all along. It would not live. A matter only, the doctor said, of time. It had been, in the end, said Cullen, an easy death.

EIGHT

On a bus that puffed its way towards the foothills of the
mountains, I made my way to her home, to see for myself
the corpse of Traudl's child. I dropped some coppers into the
box but the driver did not look at me, just clasped his bony
fingers on the wheel and focused his gaze on the road ahead.
Out of the older part of the city we trundled and through
the suburbs we passed, estates half-hidden by half-hearted
attempts at unobtrusive woodlands. We passed too along the
outskirts of the city, on past the streets of my childhood, and
on past the last, pretty places of the county, Lamb's Cross,
Stepaside village, the blue church of Kilternan, as the bus
climbed up the low hills and crossed the invisible border into
Wicklow, following the sunken road that wound through a
wild chasm the locals call The Scalp, where many thousands
of years ago large detached masses of granite had fallen and
hung precipitously on the wooded shelves on both sides of
the ravine. My eyes were drawn to the confusions of smashed
up stones and rocks that seemed to threaten at every moment
to crush the bus. Some people had built their houses in this
huge ravine, under the almost-plummeting boulders and the
broken trees and loose earth. On we went further. As the

dusk descended I sharpened my eyes, picking out here and there the electric lights of human dwellings. I wondered what constellations they would form if seen from the sky. On the bus went passing isolated buildings scattered on the hillsides, following its lonely route down the slope as the mountains rose on either side. As a boy I had always believed one of these mountains to be an extinct volcano until one day my father disabused my imaginings. *Quartzite*, he had said dismissively, *they use it for building patios*.

I stepped off the bus when it came to my stop. It was raining and I soon became wet. I snagged the coat of the navy suit on a thorn bush and a thread came loose. As I walked I could hear snail shells being crunched with each falling step. I tried picking my way more carefully but it was no use. In the dark and wet they had come out and I could not avoid killing them or at least destroying their shells. A light in the distance guided my way to the house. I walked nervously up the driveway. How many times had I crossed this threshold? All those times... but I can't.

Come in, come in, thank you so much for coming, said Traudl, opening the door, *come in, you're wet, she's in here*.

I shook Cullen's hand as he approached me in the hallway and together the three of us entered the front room of the house they had bought from her parents up there in the hills, in the one place she had always wanted to live, where she herself had lived as a girl. Yes, into that room, full of Traudl's childhood things, things not mine that had nonetheless been absorbed into my memory and become part of myself, and there, laid out on a white cloth on the coffee table, the Moses basket and the baby in it. Everywhere it seemed there were mourners sitting on chairs taken from the kitchen and the garden, who could only look and not look, who could only look elsewhere and talk loudly to dampen out the muffled sobs of the women and the shuffles of the men, who would do all they could not to look at the waxen face of the infant as it lay there stiff and unmoving. Her eyes were closed over, her long lashes seemed almost painted down her cheeks. Traudl took my hand and brought me nearer, and pointed down at the body, her eyes raw and overtipping with tears, her face crumpling up, her hand on the basket trying to rock what could not be rocked, to soothe what needed no soothing.

Traudl... I began.

Isn't she beautiful, she said quickly, and I could only agree and touch the hand of the bereaved mother, her grey eyes dampened black with crying, and kept my mouth moving as I murmured, *Yes, just beautiful*.

She looked at me up and down. *Your suit, it's a bit torn there,* she remarked, picking at the thread. *But it suits you. The beard too.* Her eyes travelled elsewhere. Traudl stroked her baby's face. *We have called her Liesl*, she said sadly.

There Liesl lay on her side, her tiny, oblong head more tiny than I had expected, the occiput garnished with rough clumps of matted, black hair, her peach skin covered in patches of whitish-grey flakes, the yellow weeds of decay already creeping through. Her swollen eyes were closed over as if they had been punched shut in the womb by a terrified mother; her ears were in the wrong place, low, triangular, dysplastic. In the middle of her face was a large cleft like one large extended nostril, through which hard whitening gums and a flat, leech-like tongue could be seen. Her rigid mouth was opened, as though expectant of something, but no teeth would ever grow there, no lover's kisses would ever be placed on her invisible lips. Overlapping fingers clenched into fists protruded out of the arm-cuffs of her white lace dress. I could not see any thumbs; she had no jaw; her neck was squashed between her head and chest. Her back was curved, a half-oval bend, and would have bent her double in time if she had lived; her little purple feet were rounded, convex, unusably bumped, like the rockers on the bottom of my grandmother's favourite chair. I touched a toe; it was icy and alien.

She was inside out, Traudl said to me as she ran the back of her finger down Liesl's scaly cheek. *All the bowels were in a sack on her belly where they had grown through her skin. Babies like this develop hernias. She would have never eaten properly and her kidneys didn't work. Her bones were so weak.*

There was a bustling noise from the hallway.

Will you excuse me, said Traudl, *I think my parents have arrived.*

I found a chair. Nobody came to speak to me.

How long did I sit there in the living room, drinking cups of tea, munching cheese and cucumber sandwiches that someone had brought, the deformed child an embarrassing presence? A matter of minutes only. I had an urge to flee but quietly fought against it. Will you not open your eyes? I silently begged Liesl. Will you not open your eyes and see the unspeakable grief that your ghastly death has caused? Somewhere Cullen was courteously accepting condolences, his voice stoic and steady and gracious. Thoughts and images unwanted came to me: death inescapable was in the midst of all, hollowing out everything once more with its reverberant presence. I sat there and ate the sandwiches, stuffing my gob until I could eat no more.

The evening wore on. I could not look at Liesl any longer; second by second her physical condition was deteriorating and soon the time would come to close the coffin and deposit her misshapen body in the earth. Traudl had disappeared somewhere. Cullen was holding long whispered conversations with people I did not know. His face was ashen, strained with anguish and emptiness. It was a father's pain; taut, disorderly, contrapuntal. I wandered into the garden and sat down under a huge cherry blossom. A strange, elemental feeling came over me. Tiredness, yes, and oddly removed, as if I was watching myself from a distance. For the first time I thought of my father's sadness in the days after I had left his house, but I did not know this grief nor its duration, its temperament, the violence it had done to him. Or perhaps he had been grateful for my leaving, had been seeking me out to thank me. Or perhaps… but perhaps nothing. Nothing could be thought that was not thought itself and yet the thoughts were wrong.

Think. Yes, for the first time I thought of my father's grief in the days after my mother's funeral. When his wife died he must have felt a great injustice had been done. Why had she not lived as they said she would? In the weeks after her death he cornered the doctors, demanding answers, but they said that they had new patients and in any case they were unable to change the facts. The doctor in charge of her case, Bixby, said he has seen hundreds of cases like it – hundreds! – and they all end the same way, one way or another. He took off his glasses and squeezed the bridge of his nose, scrunching up his eyes. *You can't take it personally*, Bixby said. It occurs to my father suddenly that only a merciless God would kill without making his reasons understood. Or perhaps he means merciful? There are no answers to his questions. He is unsure if he is even asking the right questions. Perhaps, he thought, perhaps... but perhaps nothing. And then, from somewhere forgotten, there was a splendour of images swarming up out of the abyss, of a holiday taken one Easter long ago. My father driving the car, an old red jalopy. My mother there too, in the passenger seat, looking absent-mindedly out of the window, and my sister and I, our heads resting on each other's shoulders as we drift off to sleep. I thought of him thinking of the violets and bluebells, of the orchids and hawthorns he has seen, those white cotton bushes on the side of the byways that he never knew the names of, of the lambs in the spring fields following aimlessly after the ewes, of the blaze of the sun overhead as he once lay dreaming in a half-sleep on a beach surrounded by high cliffs where gannets came and went. On the beach, the lapping water, there it begins and ends. Down on the southwest coast, where the last vestiges of another grammar dwindles in the gullets of the natives, a cove with caves on the rocks behind, and where the grassy rises, guardians of the land, abide protectively, enfolding the sunrays for the untroubled bathers down below and warming the innumerable rockpools for the crabs and the starfish and seaweed. How he loved the sun. Here he was... yes, say it, happy. His wife beside him, brushing sand from between her toes and gazing out towards the jagged islets that climbed precipitously out of the ocean. His children too, a boy and a girl, playing together in the warm rockpools, hunting for life. One day, on a whim, they had all travelled out on a boat to those sea-rocks to see the puffins and the seals, and to climb the steps that led to the summit. Monks had lived there once, a long time ago, and for longer there than most, in silence, in huts, almost all trace of the lives they had chosen now erased but for the stone hives where once been housed. They had made a prayer of their isolation, a glory of their simplicity. On the highest precipice in the rocks was a bed for the holiest monk of all, who had slept there all huddled up, vulnerable to the eye of heaven. Submissive or supplicant? His bones were discovered under the hollow of a rock, his last gesture of humility. And centuries later they had followed the monks out and remarked in fascination upon all that remained of them: hut, rock, bone.

An old woman was tugging my arm. I turned my eyes to her.

The poor mite. Only three days, cradle to coffin. What was the actual cause? she asked me.

Her heart was defective, I told her. *In the end it just gave up.*

The old woman nodded and lowered her head.

I lost my own husband that way. Just dropped dead on me one day. His heart, she said, thumping her palm forcefully into her chest, *just gave up.*

I thought; I could do nothing else but think. Thoughts came clearly to me. See my father now. Alone now he sits in the chair by the patio doors in the house in the outer suburbs off the outer ring-road, sitting there with the sun streaming through the glass and warming the room so that he feels himself lost in the haze. It doesn't last long: over and over the remembrance of his wife in a maternity ward swims up. Why this memory? Her first child, my half-forgotten sister. A weeping daughter in her arms, she was happy. How had she, who had never thought her existence unjustified, been so unjustly destroyed? The more he thinks the less he understands. No. The more he thinks the more his thinking becomes thought itself. Every thought is a question, and every day his questions harden until they become expressions of hatred against his unstoppable, furious thinking that is both evanescent and glutinous. His mind is filled with the phenomena of doubt; every object he encounters is an instrument of reproof. There in the photograph on the wall is their image, taken on their wedding day. From behind the glass, both of them smile out at him, derisory figures eternally frozen, bloodlessly enduring into perpetuity. He rages and rages about the injustice of it all until one day he is so engulfed in rage he smashes their wedding photograph against the wall. That image of happiness is now nothing more than a treacherous, degrading lie, an anti-truth. Pieces of glass shatter about the floor and the paper image of the newlyweds he tramples on becomes crumpled and dirty. He stamps his feet all over the photograph, and still the faces that are no longer theirs smile out at him. In all the confusion, a single, unwanted tear escapes from his eye.

Suddenly ashamed, he sinks to the floor and straightens out the photograph. Underneath the mucky footprints, there they are, unchanged, un-aged, still smiling youthfully at the camera. He remembers the day they got married. How beautiful she looked with her long auburn hair flowing over her pale skin. It seemed to him then that she made everything around her shimmer, now diminishing, now intensifying, now thinning, now tingling. The petals of the flowers in her hand had fluttered; he remembers how he had felt his fingers tremble when he first touched her face. They were happy. Now she was departed and her quivering world had ceased to be. Another image comes before him of his wife, cold and hard and impassive in her polished, purple velvet-lined coffin. The smell of lacquered wood. Or does he mean indifferent? She was neither defeated nor stoic but indifferent; no, that was wrong, he thought her unmoving face seemed the perfect expression of existence. At first he can't explain why he thought that thought, but then he sees all the other things around him, objects, colours, shapes, the facts of themselves which they cannot express, all those things which are cold and hard and impassive. There sits a chair, a table, a corpse. But he is wrong; they were neither cold nor hard except to him; it is he who was conferring impassiveness on them.

Stretched there his wife too was incapable of anything. Lumpy, base, useless. This death, he thought, is freakish. He thought that he could plunge his fingers into his wife's eyes, he could choke her by the neck and pull on her tongue; he even thought about trying to kiss her. But all that would have been achieved would be a violation of the stasis, a rearrangement of the facts. Left on her own to decompose the stasis would be violated anyway. Every living thing was a transgression of the settling dust, he sees that now. But no, that word is wrong; not a transgression, but an actor, in the dumb procession. And then he understands in that moment that it is not the dead who are the aberrations, but the living. Encompassed by the dead things, and the never-living things, is the pitiless event of living, he thinks. He understands now that the living imagine their struggle to be individual, to belong only to them. He read somewhere, he cannot remember where, that the whole of human thought had mistakenly accepted that the struggle of humanity was the coming to terms with selfhood. But this was only one dimension of the selfish delusion: the struggle of humans is not theirs alone, but rather it is the struggle of an un-human, unrepentant force of life against its own inevitable extinction that animates each self. It passes from generation to generation, from being to being, and each atomised being is born a host for that struggle. It is indiscriminate, and although it is not human, humans feel it as their own-most fate. What is thinking but the pressing out of this force? Each thought a thinning out of the drip-dropping hours.

On the walls of his home there are photographs of his wife, his children and his father and mother, his whole extended family; each one possessing the force of life which unwittingly passed into him and through him. The deceased are each one of them a tattered skeleton, exhausted of the force that grew their flesh and then tore it apart. Now all that remains of them is their human image on a yellowed scrap of paper. This force is too slowly exhausting itself of him, he understands. Yes, he realises that clearly now. He did not realise it at the time, but his contribution to the generations was all involuntary. His daughter, who like his son has fled his house now, yes, just like his son, whom he loved more than anything else he had ever known, was an outcome of a frenzy of energy which had made him feel powerful, and in the marvel of sexual expulsion he imagined he felt the indestructible core of his being. This is what it feels to be a man, he had said to himself as he collapsed down on top of his wife. He lay in the dark, listening to his wife's breathing and thinking of the seed he had planted in her. He momentarily harboured a notion of himself as a creator, bringing into existence something which had never been before. Powerful, potent, man the life-giver. But now he sees the error, he should have wished to be impotent. He thought his children would be a legacy of his unique existence but each one was a further assault on the only sovereignty he possesses. Each child born was an assault on the only resistance he could have mustered; each child making him a vassal of nature.

But no, that was wrong too, for it was not nature that made him a slave. This force was not nature; nature was the impoverished struggle of one form of life against another. The blooming tree, the hatching fish, the new-born human child, each one the foot soldier blindly marching in the service of an unseen and unseeing power, fighting against nothing but the gum of nothingness. Existence he had thought the same as life; and all the living things were privileged. Nature, he had once told his young son, awakens itself through the eyes of humanity. He read that somewhere, he couldn't remember where, a German or a Greek had said it. He thinks perhaps that death is true existence; and in that case everything living was raging against this state of static being, bringing about its entropy, the universe moving towards stillness. It matters not: he believes now he is nothing more than the disposable vessel of a blind, indiscriminate vitality. He hates being used in this way. He no longer knows how or why to live. Grief swells up in the hollows inside him: the more he tries to understand his grief the less authentic it feels; the more he succumbs to his grief the less he understands of the world. He wishes most of all that he could stop these unstoppable thoughts and yet remain alive. His head is full of questions for which there are no answers, and in all the questions he does not know which is the right question to ask. He decides to act in the only moral way he can. He will kill his only son and take possession of himself again. He takes up a pillow to smother him; he can almost hear the beating of his son's heart. I picture him hovering over me as I sleep, listening to my breathing. He has broken into my flat to kill me, his eyes filled with hatred and resentment, for in killing his son he will renounce the only demand that nature has ever made of him. In killing his son he will recoup whatever is left of his now jaded autonomy. But the pillow in his hand is as weightless as a soul. He looks at me, his mind blazoned with fear and terror. Though he has murder in his heart and an insuperable urge to destroy this child of his, which though of him has abandoned him a little more day by day since his birth, he is paralysed by love and by pity. He is full of bitterness too, and yet his courage fails him. Always cowardice, he thinks, always too late. Everything feels out of equilibrium, he becomes dizzy and grasps at the bed to stay upright, before he lands on the floor with a crash, gazing upwards at the ceiling, his heart beating, and beating on and on until the moment when his heart will beat out its final feverish threnody, his blood stilled at last.

The image of my father faded, and became the memory of an image. I had told myself a story about him; it was not the story he would have told. I felt a warm hand on my arm. Traudl was there, tracing weary fingers across my skin. On a bench under the splendid pink flowers of the cherry blossom she sat beside me, the evening breeze blowing softly against our faces. I tried to say something but Traudl put a finger to her lips and her sorrow-reddened eyes pleaded for quiet. The mountains loomed behind us, their forests imperious in their black silence. Up those rocky paths we had wandered, up to the top to stand on the rocks to look out over the city and the sea. I thought of Traudl and me in that moon-silvered mountain glade where we had lain down and kneaded together our hips on the plush, pine-scented floor until we sank into the incommensurable depths of human fulfilment. The time for that was past; now the heart was drained and the womb was empty. The time too for saying these things was long past. Now she rested her drowsy head on my shoulder and turned her eyes skyward, where dark figures were restlessly flittering. There, above our heads, tens, maybe hundreds, maybe a thousand, I do not know these things, I have never known these things, of blue-black-winged swallows were in the fullness of their evening ballet, forked tails and sharpened wings slicing through the air, their cream and rust heads swiftly darting through the dark orange glow with mysterious, avian purpose. They had made this place their transitory home and in a few weeks it would be time to gather the flocks for the long migration south once more, where many would perish on the way, fall from their flight to the earth and seas below. For a long time it seemed we watched them as they rose and fell, and once more rose and fell, their numbers dwindling one by one, until they all came to rest in the eaves of the shed in Traudl's garden.

It had been, in the end, a simple burial. Cullen carried in his outstretched arms the miniature box up the sloping hill of the cemetery. Traudl by his side. A small hole had been dug in the ground; it did not take long to lower the coffin. The gravediggers stood nearby, elbows resting conspicuously on shovels, fags burning under the eyeless peaks of their caps. In another part of the cemetery a small funeral was taking place. A mourner remarked on the quality of the white wood Liesl's coffin had been made from, but nobody responded. Somewhere else colours were changing second by second on the faces of the newly deceased, colours that could not be seen nor imagined. Many hands were clasped and unclasped. Small conversations broke out and faded away just as quickly. We stood there for less than an hour until those assembled began to shuffle off one by one or in groups of twos and threes.

I followed an elderly man down the hill, keeping an eye on his surefooted heels. He kept his head down, his eyes picking out the safest parts of the stony pathway. Sorrowful words were being uttered behind me, growing more distant with each step.

Goodbye Liesl, said Traudl.

Goodbye Liesl, said Cullen, *my darling girl, my darling girl*.

Near the bottom of the hill men in black were waiting, as I knew they would be, their hands hooked respectfully behind their backs, the faces directed towards the void. In a long black hearse, a driver with dark glasses turned over the engine, and beside him sat a small man with a ruddy face and a bowler hat, a fist in his hand, chewing a finger, choosing his moment. And there, behind the hearse, was a tall man, his red eyes on the scene, watching, waiting. A crow cawed and something began to turn in my stomach. They stood there observing, stealing inches, these shades of men, passing over the mourners as they left the graveyard. I knew that soon they would come for me too.

Yes: soon they would come, of that much I was certain, I saw it clearly. The clock will tick on in the bedroom. I might pick up my pen or call Schorman – but no, I do not have the heart for that any more. No more of that. Time will pass. In the dusk, birds will gather on the telephone wires, their eyes cocked impassively at and away from my window. The constellations will rise and turn, Draco huge and silent. The clock will tick on. The sound of footsteps then, clearer, louder, slowly pacing outside on the stone. I will creep over to the window, dragging my feet across the carpet in trepidation. Through the netting a figure there, peering up at my window through the gloom. A man. Yes, most certainly a man. Was there to be no rest? Was there, in the end, to be no reward? Find the matches and strike a flame, burn the envelope and the last remains of the money, the final payment. Footsteps then on the little concrete bridge to the black door. A bolt sliding down and the black door opening. Stand up and reach for the doorknob, feel once more its cold and inhuman form. Footsteps then on the stairs, softly treading the newly laid carpet underneath. Breathe slower and tighten the grip. The door opening, carefully, ghostly, come then to a halfway halt. The inside of my chest hammering, as if it will try to frantically empty itself of itself. No movement outside. In the darkness there, shapeless sound. Forms forming, creeping forward. Shades of men everywhere, men in suits, men in rags. Objects still about me, mute, surrounding, disregarding. Black figures flitting, rising and hovering above. Mother protect me. Everywhere light then in the radiance of the dead. Everything dead then in the pure time of the living. Neither one of us crossing the threshold. In my heart, beating furiously, I will know who it is.

I turned away coldly and continued my descent down the hill. I left the cemetery with the red eyes trained on my back and in spite of my best efforts I felt my pace quicken. I realised I had nowhere to go. I thought briefly about going back to the park but I quickly put that idea out of my mind. The sun had risen steadily. I wandered up a country road until I found an old stone wall under a tree to sit on. I sat there for a while calming myself and looking up at the clouds, which were changing minute by minute. Soon Cullen would drive Traudl home to begin their life anew. The sun was almost at its highest point of the day. The warmth had brought out little blood-red spider mites who were swarming all over the concrete wall. I crushed a few of them under my thumb but there were too many to destroy.

There was nothing left to do except to go home.